An Ominous Death

An Ominous Death

Annette Mahon

Five Star • Waterville, Maine

First Edition
First Printing: February 2006

Published in 2006 in conjunction
with Tekno Books and Ed Gorman.

Set in 11 pt. Plantin by Elena Picard.

Printed in the United States on permanent paper.

Library of Congress Cataloging-in-Publication Data

Mahon, Annette.
    An ominous death / by Annette Mahon.—1st ed.
      p. cm.
    ISBN 1-59414-359-5 (hc : alk. paper)
    1. Women private investigators—Fiction. 2. Quiltmakers —Fiction. 3. Older women—Fiction. 4. Scottsdale (Ariz.) —Fiction. I. Title.
PS3563.A3595O46 2006
813′.54—dc22   2005028625

For my fellow muses,
Deni, Garda, Harriet, Lillian,
Mary Jo, Sherry-Anne, and Terey.
I can't thank you enough for always being there
with your support and encouragement.
Without y'all, this book may not have made it.

Acknowledgements

With special thanks to those who answered my numerous questions in the writing of this book: Nelson Lapan and Mark Ruffennach of the Scottsdale Police Department, Dr. Ted Rudberg, Dr. Doug Lyle, and Mary Welk.

The jelous Swan, ayenst hys deth that singeth,
the Oule eke, that of deth the bode bringeth.
　　　　—Chaucer, *Assembly of Foules*

The screech-owl, with ill-boding cry,
Portends strange things, old women say;
Stops every fool that passes by,
And frights the school-boy from his play.
—Lady Mary Wortley Montagu, *The Politicians*

It is the owl that shrieked, the fatal bellman
Which gives the stern'st good-night.
　　　—William Shakespeare, *Macbeth*

Owl, owl, burrowing owl with their eyes
each other relishing,
Owl, owl, burrowing owl with their eyes
each other relishing,
Whomever's child is a crybaby, we will eat.
Not you while crying, then go to sleep,
not you will I eat.
Then you while crying go to sleep, you will I eat.
　　　　—Hopi lullaby

Prologue

Candy lay in the darkness, eyes open, ears alert. Quiet footsteps sounded in the hall. A cold sweat filmed her forehead as fear rippled through her. A sudden and urgent need to visit the bathroom added to her already enormous discomfort.

Candy watched the door; her breath halted to better enable her to listen. The strip of light beneath the door shadowed and her heart startled so violently she thought surely it would stop. Then, like a cloud before the sun, the shadow passed and she could once again see the long stripe of the hall light beneath the door. The steps receded. In a minute she heard the stealthy sound of a door open and close.

There was a door in that direction that led outside. She might be trapped in this room by her heavy leg casts, but she'd been given the grand tour, and her memory was as good as ever. There were three more rooms past hers—all occupied—and a door leading out onto the grounds. The attendant had gone that way when she took her out in the wheel chair the other day, to sit in the garden for a short while during the cooler morning temperatures.

Candy took a deep, shaky breath. She held it for a full minute while her ears strained for any sound. She heard the hum of the air conditioners, a deep rumble that sounded through the building at a steady and uninterrupted rate.

Somewhere nearby a faucet opened and closed, the water running noisily through the pipes. Faintly, she heard the ring of a telephone, probably out at the nurse's office. She couldn't make out any voices. And there were definitely no more footsteps. Relief, however, did not come.

Would this night be a safe one then? Or would she awaken to find a shadowy figure looming over her bed? Or another new acquaintance gone?

Candy lay in the darkness for a long time before she finally succumbed to exhaustion and slept.

1

"I heard that Candy Breckner has moved into the Palo Verde Care Center," Maggie Browne commented. Candy, an active member of the St. Rose Senior Guild, was an intermittent member of the Quilting Bee.

"Care center!" Edie Dulinski sniffed. "Just a fancy word for a nursing home. Lets them charge more."

There were two nods and a raised eyebrow, but everyone continued to stitch. Work was progressing nicely on the Bee's latest quilt, a blue and white nine-patch.

"I spoke with Violet Dawson yesterday." Maggie drew her thread through the quilt sandwich and smoothed the line of stitching with her finger. "She lives near Candy, you know, and she told me."

Once again Edie sniffed. "Candy! Such an inappropriate name for an old woman."

Anna Howard, who had been ready to question Maggie about Candy, turned instead to Edie. "Really, Edie. She didn't have any say in what she was named, now did she?"

Maggie tried not to grin. Although Edie's comments often rubbed her the wrong way, she had to admit that in this case Edie had a point. Candy Breckner looked nothing like the woman Maggie pictured when she heard that name. A "Candy" should have soft, plump cheeks and a face with an eternally childish aspect. Or perhaps a grandmotherly woman with a cushiony lap. But Candy Breckner was a small, thin, sharp-featured woman, often compared to Margaret Hamilton, the actress who had played the witch in the classic *Wizard of Oz* movie.

With a small shake of her head, Maggie returned her attention to her sewing, and to the conversation.

"Surely Candy is a nickname," Edie was saying. "She should have gone back to her real name. It must be Candace or Caroline or something of that sort."

"Oh, no, I happen to know her given name is Candy," Clare Patterson said. "I remember her saying once that the priest gave her mother a hard time when she was baptized. He wanted her first and middle names reversed."

Edie's reply was another sniff. Maggie was beginning to wonder if she was just bothered by allergies rather than reacting to the conversation.

"In any case," Maggie said, "Candy is moving to the care facility this week."

"So they aren't letting her go home?" Anna's forehead crinkled in concern.

"I saw in the paper that an older woman was attacked over the weekend," Edie informed them. "Two men walked right in her house and knocked her out, then stole all her money and jewelry. Right there in Candy's neighborhood. That used to be such a nice area." Edie shook her head. "A woman with two leg casts would be a sitting duck."

"Honestly, Edie." Maggie frowned at the other woman. While an expert needlewoman, Edie had the disconcerting habit of expounding on disasters of all sorts. Local crime was a particular favorite, as was the danger they were all in, even in their own homes, in these unsettled times.

"Well, you are right about one thing," Maggie reluctantly agreed. She turned back toward the others; her fingers still busy plying her needle. "Candy certainly can't go home with two broken legs, Anna. How would she manage?"

Candy had had an auto accident the week before. Driving home from her daughter's house after a family party celebrating her grandchildren's birthday, she'd lost control of her car and hit a stone wall. The small sporty car Candy was so proud of had been smashed beyond repair, but she escaped with her life and both her legs broken.

"Couldn't her family help?" Victoria Farrington turned an inquiring look toward Maggie. "Couldn't someone stay with her?"

"You've heard her talk about her daughter," Maggie responded. "Remember how proud Candy was when she opened that store? And then when she made such a success of it? But owning a small retail shop is a demanding job."

Clare nodded. "Candy has every right to be proud. Andrea was businesswoman of the year last year."

"And don't forget she has those twins," Anna put in.

There was a moment of silence. Maggie knew that the others, like herself, were reflecting on the fact that Candy had been hurt after leaving the twins' birthday party.

Louise snipped a thread and reached for the spool. "Candy talks a lot about how easily her daughter juggles family and work responsibilities. But I always wonder . . ."

Her new thread inserted into the needle, knotted and ready, Louise took a moment to set the knot into the quilt sandwich. She spoke again once she began stitching. "These young women take on so much, I'm not always sure they handle it as well as they pretend."

"I guess that's why she can't take care of her mother," Anna said. "With a business and a family, it would be difficult for her to look after a convalescing parent as well."

Edie sniffed. "You'd think she'd make an effort. Young people have no sense of family responsibility these days."

"It would be awfully hard for her to handle a woman with two leg casts," Louise told her. "I'm sure she would do it otherwise. I seem to recall she's very close to her mother."

"What about her stepchildren?" Anna asked.

"I don't think she was very close to them," Victoria said.

"She wasn't," Clare said. It was Clare's turn to snip off her thread and reach for the spool. "She was always going on about the twins, but I know both Nathan and Stephanie have children and Candy hardly ever mentioned them."

"You're making her sound like the evil stepmother," Louise said, one side of her mouth pulling down.

"I didn't mean to." Clare deftly sank her knot into the quilt and continued to stitch. "But she'd only been married to Ken for a few years when he passed away. His children were already fully grown and had families of their own by then. She made them quilts and all. I remember the sailboat quilt she made for Stephanie's little boy. She just didn't fuss about them like she did the twins."

They all stitched in silence for a moment.

"We should all go out to see her," Maggie suggested.

"What a good idea," Victoria agreed. "We could carpool from here—maybe tomorrow?"

"We should do it next week," Anna said. "That way we can make a small quilt over the weekend to take over for her. Something to throw over her lap and hide those casts."

Everyone loved the idea and talk immediately turned to quilt patterns. Maggie smiled as she listened to her friends debate these weighty issues. She loved this group. Even Edie, behind all that grumbling and pessimism, had a good heart.

After several minutes of lively discussion weighing the pros and cons of various patterns, everyone agreed that as they were working on a nine-patch, they should make some nine-patch blocks for Candy's lap quilt. They were also simple to do, so could be stitched quickly.

"We can tie it, and she'll have a nice quilt to put over her legs when she watches television with the other patients," Anna said.

"If we do the blocks right away, and you all give them to me, I'll machine quilt it over the weekend," Edie offered.

"That's terrific." Maggie smiled at Edie. "You do such nice machine quilting, certainly much better than mine."

"I think we should alternate the nine-patch blocks with appliquéd hearts," Victoria suggested.

"We can sign the heart blocks," Louise added.

By the time the Bee put away their sewing things at the end of the morning, they had decided to have lunch together at Maggie's and begin the work on Candy's quilt. Then they would carpool to the care center to visit their friend the following Monday.

2

The Palo Verde Care Center was located a short five miles from St. Rose Catholic Church, an older parish in the southern part of Scottsdale, where the Quilting Bee met. The St. Rose Quilting Bee was part of the St. Rose Senior Guild that met every morning for companionship and crafts. St. Rose's pastor, Father Bob O'Connell, had decided some years ago to offer activities for his increasing number of newly retired parishioners. So he'd created the Senior Guild, whose members met each morning and produced a multitude of craft items for an annual Halloween Craft Fair. The quilts made by the Quilting Bee were auctioned off in an event that drew bidders from across the nation. And each year there was a raffle quilt—the last quilt they made, just before the grand event. It was always an appliquéd rose pattern, always exquisite.

Candy Breckner was an active member of the St. Rose Senior Guild, but only a sometime member of the Quilting Bee. Candy always said that she thrived on variety, and so she moved about among the various groups. When not quilting with the Bee, she might embroider silk ribbon flowers on receiving blankets, or stitch doll clothes with the needleworkers. She'd smocked aprons and little girl's dresses, and needlepointed tissue box covers. But the Bee members thought of her as one of their own, so they were all present on the day of the visit to give her the lap quilt they had made.

The care center was in an older neighborhood, green with mature trees and irrigated lawns. The center itself was a large Mediterranean style building located on the spacious grounds where an elementary school had once stood. As the population of the city migrated north, schools were constantly being added in the areas flooded with new subdivisions. But in the older neighborhoods to the south, attendance had been falling and more than one school had been closed. Palo Verde Elementary School had been gone for over fifteen years.

"I've never been here before," Victoria said as Louise drove into the parking area at the Palo Verde Care Center. Louise had been elected to drive, as she owned a van that would comfortably seat all six Bee members. "They certainly did a nice job with the grounds."

The others looked at the large green lawn edged with shade-giving eucalyptus, mulberry, pine and sumac trees. Plots of blooming flowers provided spots of bright color. Standing guard between the parking area and the main garden was a venerable old olive tree with a gnarled trunk at least five feet around. The Bee women could see patients sitting outside, some in wheel chairs, some on benches under the trees. The entire lot was surrounded by a beautifully worked wrought iron fence painted the same beige as the stucco building.

"It's smart of them to put up a fence like that," Edie announced from the back seat. "You never know who might be roaming around these days, even in the nicer neighborhoods."

"Hmm," Maggie murmured. "But is it to keep people out?" she asked. "Or in?"

3

Candy was overwhelmed by her friends' visit. Tears streamed down her cheeks as she spread the nine-patch over her lap, thanking them with fluttering smiles and stuttering words.

Finally, she wiped her tears. Running her hand over one of the red appliquéd hearts, her index finger traced the line of Maggie's signature. "And it's red, white and blue. You all remembered how much I like patriotic colors."

"We're quilting a blue nine-patch right now," Clare told her. "You might be back in time to put in a few stitches before we finish it."

"I'll think of all of you stitching on it every time I see this," Candy promised. "Oh, it's so good to see you." Candy dabbed at her eyes, but the action was fruitless as tears continued to flow.

Victoria pulled her chair closer to Candy's wheelchair and patted her hand. "Now you just settle down and we'll have a nice chat. How are you feeling?"

Candy took a deep breath and dabbed once again at her damp cheeks. "Oh, I'm not too bad. The doctor says I'll be back to all my old activities in no time at all."

There were exclamations from the others at this, and comments on how they would look forward to seeing her back at the Senior Guild.

"What's that you're working on?" Edie asked, indicating a bit of canvas half covered by the quilt in Candy's lap.

Candy frowned, but reached for the canvas and pulled it out. She spread out a partially worked needlepoint canvas showing a grouping of colorful irises.

"I told Andrea to bring me something to work on. I'd wanted her to bring my latest quilting project. I've been doing some patriotic redwork blocks—they're the block of the month at the quilt store this year. I'm behind on them, but I have all the patterns traced onto the muslin and in my sewing basket." Candy sighed. "She went over to my place and came back with this. Said she doesn't know her way around a sewing room." Candy shook her head. "She can keep track of every bit of inventory in that store of hers, but she can't tell the difference between quilting blocks and needlepoint canvas." With a frown, Candy flicked the canvas. "I don't know where she found this. But all the yarn and needles are here and it's something to do with my hands. It's so frustrating not being able to get around."

The others commiserated with her. Maggie was horrified by the thought of being caught in a wheelchair like Candy. Imagine being unable to drive a car or to ride a horse. Maggie was used to being on the go; she thought she understood the frustration evident in Candy's voice. Being confined to this one room, nice as it was—and without her pet projects!

"This is a lovely place," Anna commented, as conversation lulled. There was a large window in Candy's room, and Anna sat before it. The view was charming, of the gardens they had glimpsed from the parking lot. "Such beautiful gardens."

Poor Anna. Her simple comment caused a reaction in Candy that startled them all.

Candy began to wail—there was no other word for it—deep sobs ripping from her chest.

Anna's eyes were wide, horrified at this response to her attempt at small talk. While Victoria handed Candy a box of tissues from the night stand, Maggie reached over to pat Anna's hand. Louise moved up beside Candy and rubbed her back. It seemed to help.

Finally, Candy took a deep breath. It vibrated in her throat, made her cough. Then she took another, more normal breath and spoke.

"I thought it was a lovely place too, at first. But this is a terrible place, terrible." Her voice was hushed, hoarse from her recent crying; it dropped in volume as she spoke, until it was a mere whisper at the end.

Amazed, her friends stared, momentarily at a loss for words. Louise, still standing beside Candy's wheelchair, poured out a glass of water from a bottle beside the bed and handed it to her. Candy sipped, then cleared her throat. She seemed more like her usual self.

Maggie's eyes met Louise's for a brief moment. What could have gotten into Candy?

Edie was the first to recover. "What's wrong, Candy? Don't they treat you well?"

Maggie, who had had the same thought, did a visual check of Candy. Sitting in a wheelchair, Candy was dressed simply in a loose-fitting, navy blue dress. She wore a light-weight sweater over it, pale pink with ribbon embroidery along the neckline. There were a few bruises on her hands and face, but Maggie felt sure these were caused by the air bag deploying during her accident. The rest of her body was covered by her clothes, the casts, and the friendship quilt they'd brought.

Sometimes, it's the small things that really matter,

Maggie thought, as she glanced over Candy again. The other woman's hair was nicely arranged in the French twist she favored. She wore no makeup, but then she didn't usually wear more than a little lipstick. Maggie noticed that a tube of lipstick sat on the bedside table, along with a small mirror that Candy could use to apply it. Her hands, both of which were wrapped around the water glass, showed nails recently manicured and painted with a shell pink polish.

Candy looked comfortable and well groomed, and her room was lovely. The staff they'd seen on the way in seemed efficient and friendly.

Maggie exchanged a look with Louise, who seemed to be completing her own inventory of Candy's appearance. Next to the well-padded figure of Louise, Candy appeared painfully thin, but that was her natural state.

Louise shrugged, with a slight shake of her head. So she hadn't seen anything either that might clue them in on why Anna's comment might have caused such a severe reaction. And with her experience of hospitals and care facilities, Louise should have more insight into the situation than the rest of them.

Maggie turned her attention back to Candy. They spent a few more minutes calming her down. After that, it didn't take much urging for Candy to tell them what was troubling her. However, she spoke in a voice so soft, those farther from her chair had to strain to hear. She even insisted on putting on the radio first—to help cover the sound of her voice, she said.

"Do you think someone is bugging your room?" Maggie smiled, indulging her friend in her little joke.

But to her surprise, Candy did not take it as a joke. Her voice and expression were dead serious. "He might be. Who knows? They didn't say anything about that on the show, but you never know these days." She glanced quickly around the room before looking back at her friends. "They make cameras and recorders so tiny, who can tell?"

The others were caught now, intrigued by this surprising side of their old friend. Maggie frowned at her, wondering if the accident had caused some strange mental problem in Candy. Could one of those bruises on her face be more serious than it appeared? Or perhaps she was on pain medication that produced paranoia or hallucinations.

"I've been here five days now," Candy began. "At first I thought the same thing you did." Her eyes met Anna's. "Gee, what a nice place. The rooms are cheery, and that beautiful garden." She glanced out the window. A hummingbird hovered briefly above the honeysuckle shrub on the other side of the glass, then did an abrupt pirouette and flew away.

Candy turned back into the room. "The food is pretty good, much better than I'd expected. They have a dietitian who comes and talks to you, and there's a dining room if you want to eat with everyone."

Candy paused, looking as though she might begin to cry again. Victoria patted her hand, encouraging her to continue.

"Some of the more ambulatory patients came to see me, and it was very nice. We visited. I began making friends."

She paused once more, but this time her demeanor was fearful. She blinked rapidly a few times and dabbed at her cheeks even though there were no tears.

"Remember Jane Madison?" she asked. "Wonderful woman. Always comes to the Halloween Bazaar. She was here."

Maggie listened to the verb tense with dread. She hoped Candy only meant that Jane had gone home, but something about Candy's tone left her thinking otherwise. Maggie did remember Jane, a plump and pleasant woman who lived near the church. At least year's Bazaar, Jane said she was still working, manning the reference desk at the Scottsdale library; but she told them she meant to join the Bee just as soon as she retired.

"Why was she here?" Anna asked.

"She had a heart attack, but was recovering well." Candy nodded at the surprised comments that came from the others. "It was a real shock to her. So young. She was only fifty-two. And all her family back in Chicago."

"Oh, my." Anna was all sympathy.

"Probably high cholesterol," Edie suggested. "She's too heavy."

Candy shrugged. "She did admit to a lifetime of eating the wrong foods. She said hamburgers and doughnuts were her downfall."

Maggie had to smile. Candy was so obviously bewildered by Jane's admitted weaknesses. With her pencil thin figure, Candy had probably never experienced a wild craving for a hamburger or a doughnut. We should all be so lucky, Maggie thought.

Candy cleared her throat.

"Jane and I got along so well." Wistfulness colored her voice. "Then she died."

Candy was whispering again, though Maggie didn't understand why. It was a shame about Jane, but she failed to see why the fact that she had died would warrant this espionage-like behavior. It was sad, but not strange. She was recovering from a heart attack, after all. She admitted to years of what was obviously the exact opposite of a heart-healthy diet.

"What a shame," Victoria said, her soothing voice an obvious balm to Candy. "How did she die?"

Candy continued to whisper. "They *said* it was another heart attack." For a moment, Candy shut her mouth; her lips pulled tight, a rebellious look on her face. "But she was doing so well. She was going home at the end of the week." Candy's voice broke and she barely managed to stifle a sob. "She'd promised to come back and visit."

"Still," Louise told her, "heart attacks can strike at any time, and quite unexpectedly."

"But there have been others." Candy's voice was obstinate, but dropped even lower. She might be convinced something was happening, but she was afraid to let others hear of it.

Maggie leaned forward. Louise took a step, moving closer to the wheelchair. "Others who had heart attacks?"

Candy nodded. "My friend, Rhonda, was here for a long time and she told me a lot of people have been dying recently. More than in all the time she'd been here."

Candy looked around, then leaned forward confidentially. Maggie found herself looking around the room as well, though it still contained only the seven women. The door into the hall was ajar, but no one was visible out there either.

Candy continued. "Rhonda, Jane and I watched this program together the night Jane died. It was one of those magazine shows on television—you know the ones."

They all nodded. Candy's voice had edged up in volume, and they were no longer straining to hear.

"It was a very interesting program. All about this man in California who worked in a nursing home and . . ."

Candy's voice dropped again and she looked nervously toward the door. Once again Maggie found herself following the other woman's glance. Through the slit of the open doorway, one person was now in sight. A frail, elderly man with a walker was working his way slowly down the hall. A tall young man in blue scrubs walked beside him.

Candy waited until they were no longer visible. When she continued, she spoke so softly Maggie resorted to watching her lips to be sure she heard her correctly. She noticed the others lean in closer, their eyes also trained on Candy's mouth.

"They called him an Angel of Death. He was killing the people there that were really sick. He thought he was helping them pass on without pain. He gave them some drug that made it look like they died of a heart attack. They never would have caught him at all except that one victim's husband started asking questions and one thing led to another." Candy finished with a firm nod.

Maggie stared at Candy. She could see that the others looked as stunned as she felt. Even Edie seemed beyond commenting.

"So what are you trying to say here?" Maggie thought she knew what Candy was implying, but it was so extraordinary she wanted to hear it stated—preferably in words of one syllable.

Candy met her gaze. "We thought maybe something like that could be going on here." Her voice, still low, broke on the word "that."

"Honestly, Candy. That's got to be the most foolish thing I ever heard!" Although the words were harsh, Louise's voice was gentle, one friend teasing another into admitting she had gone too far.

Maggie was surprised. Louise could be outspoken, true, but even spoken in that jollying tone, the tactless reply seemed unlike her. Unless she felt the unsympathetic words would jolly Candy out of her apparent paranoia.

"Louise Lombard, that was not a nice thing to say." Candy was once again near tears. "You're not trapped in here, unable to move. How do you know there's not a killer on the loose?"

Maggie could see that Louise was trying hard to say what she felt she had to without upsetting Candy.

"Oh, pooh! Just listen to yourself, Candy. 'A killer on the loose.' 'Trapped.' " Louise laughed lightly. "You sound like a heroine in a Gothic novel."

"A Gothic novel?"

Candy almost shouted the words. Her face turned bright red, and her eyes bulged. Maggie was seriously worried for her health. Apparently, so was Louise.

"Now, Candy." Louise tried to pat her arm, but Candy was having none of it. "I'm just trying to tell you what others will say. It's not logical."

But Candy was beyond reasoning. No longer soft, her voice could probably be heard all the way out at the front desk.

"You just get out of here, Louise Lombard. Out!"

Her lips pressed firmly together, Candy stared at Louise until the other woman shrugged and headed for the door.

"And don't come back," Candy shouted.

A nurse looked in, apparently alerted by Candy's loud voice. Her eyes widened as she saw Candy's condition and she stepped into the room.

"Now, Mrs. Breckner. Try to calm down."

But before the nurse had time to do more than pass the threshold, Candy shouted at her too.

"You get out too!"

Apparently deciding that listening to her patient might be best in this instance, the nurse retreated. Maggie shook her head. It was obvious the young woman was intimidated by Candy. She's much too young, Maggie thought. She'll need a lot more maturity to stand up to her patients. Maggie just hoped they would be able to calm Candy before she had a serious problem.

"No one understands," Candy muttered. Tears were streaming down her cheeks. "No one believes me."

Maggie tried to adopt a conciliatory tone. "Why don't you tell us more about it, Candy."

Temporarily mollified, Candy sniffed a few times and blew her nose. "Rhonda had been here for a long time. She was in the early stages of Alzheimer's."

Maggie exchanged a look with Victoria. They both noted the past tense Candy was using and could imagine where this was heading. But Maggie also wondered how mentally competent a woman with dementia could be—even in the earliest stages.

"Rhonda told me about other patients who died suddenly. Mostly of heart attacks. Too many, she thought, to be just random incidents. She said she tried to ask the nurses about it, but no one would talk to her." Candy choked back a sob, raising the tissue still in her hand to her mouth. "And then she died. Last night."

The Quilting Bee members stared at Candy. Looks were exchanged, a few eyebrows raised. Even Edie, that repository of newspaper crime stories, was silent.

"Was it a heart attack?" Victoria finally asked.

Candy nodded. "That's what the nurse said. But Rhonda told me herself that the doctor said her heart was strong."

Maggie reminded herself that Candy had just lost her friend and was obviously distraught. But that didn't preclude trying to reason with her—despite her treatment of Louise.

"You said neither Jane nor Rhonda was really sick," Maggie reminded her. "So why would someone want to kill them—assuming that the same thing is happening here, that is. You said this person on the program was performing mercy killings on terminally ill people."

Candy's voice dropped to a whisper once more. "I heard someone out there last night." She nodded toward her door, to the left of it. "I was so upset about this whole thing I couldn't sleep. And around one I heard someone in the hall. He was creeping along out there and my heart almost stopped." She put the tissue to her lips for a moment. "Nobody moves like that unless they're up to no good." She ended with a firm nod.

Edie was nodding with her. "That does sound suspicious," she agreed. "Most nursing people move briskly, don't you think?"

Edie looked around at the others, who were forced to agree. Experience told them that personnel in hospitals and nursing homes usually were strapped for time and moved quickly and with purpose.

"And Rhonda's room was that way?" Maggie inquired.

Candy nodded and her eyes filled with tears once more. "There's a special wing for the Alzheimer's patients, but Rhonda wasn't ill enough to be there. Most of the time she was fine. She just didn't remember things very well."

Maggie and Victoria exchanged another look. Didn't Candy realize that she was providing the perfect reason not to believe what Rhonda had suggested? If her memory was so faulty, how could Candy credit her stories about sudden, unexpected deaths?

"There are a lot of elderly patients here." Victoria's voice was soft and soothing. "Isn't it possible that they are succumbing to heart problems?"

30

"Maybe," Candy reluctantly agreed. "But doesn't it seem strange to you that all these people are dying here in a care facility? We're all supposed to be here to recover from various injuries and surgeries. If we were fatally ill, we would still be in the hospital. Why are so many people dying?"

"That does seem like a good question," Victoria agreed. "You should be able to ask the management about it. It seems like the kind of thing a potential client would want to know."

"Oh, I couldn't." Candy looked so fearful the women quickly reassured her that they would not go to the management with any questions. "He might find out."

No one bothered to inquire who "he" might be. They all knew it was Candy's so-called Angel of Death.

"You should have your family look into it though," Maggie told her.

Victoria agreed. "Isn't your daughter's husband a lawyer? Have him ask a few questions."

"Oh, he's not that kind of lawyer. He does taxes or trusts or something." Candy waved her hand vaguely.

Maggie, whose own oldest son was a contract lawyer, dismissed this. "Doesn't matter. All you need is to have him say he's a lawyer, and ask a few questions. Or write them a note on his letterhead. You'd be surprised what you can learn when you have a lawyer ask."

Clare nodded. "It scares people thinking that you've hired a lawyer. They pay attention then."

"That's what I'm afraid of," Candy said. She looked ready to cry again. "I don't want them to pay attention to me. I just want to go home." A quick glance down to the quilt on her lap and the ends of the casts it covered caused her to sob. "But I know Andrea is too busy with her family and her job to take me in."

Maggie frowned. It was a sad fact of modern life that this should be so. Young families these days were all two-income families, and they couldn't manage on one. Care facilities like this one were in business because families could no longer care for their older members when they became ill. Though, to be fair, she had to admit that it would be difficult to handle Candy's care even if her daughter didn't work. A woman with two broken legs, two heavy casts . . . Even though Andrea was taller than her mother, Maggie doubted she would be able to care for her—even if she had the time.

"I'm sure Andrea's husband doesn't want me to move in with them either. Alan's never liked me," Candy said with a sigh. "And Nathan and Stephanie don't care about me at all."

Maggie didn't think her jaw dropped, but Anna's certainly did. And Maggie didn't think she'd ever seen Victoria's eyebrows rise so high. Even Clare, that eager gossip, looked vaguely embarrassed. She fidgeted in her plastic chair, almost sending it toppling.

But Edie was the real surprise. Her lips tightened, but she remained silent.

"Candy," Maggie began. "I'm sure your stepchildren care about you."

"How would you know," Candy snapped. "Don't you start on me, Maggie Browne, or you can just go join Louise out in the car. Those children of Ken's have always resented me."

The Bee women exchanged glances. Although no words were spoken, they knew each other well enough to realize it was time to go. No one wanted to debate with Candy about her stepchildren.

Maggie put her hand on Candy's arm. "You're getting tired," she said, hoping the other woman wouldn't refute her. "It's time for us to go. We'll be coming to visit again though."

"Thank you for coming." Candy swiped a tissue across her eyes and tried to look brave. "And for my lovely quilt." Her hands ran over the fabric of the lap quilt.

Maggie and the others stood. Maggie retrieved the needlepoint canvas from the floor near Candy's wheelchair, placing it in her lap.

"Here you go, Candy. This must have fallen."

Another tear ran down Candy's cheek. "Thank you, Maggie. I wouldn't have been able to get it myself. It's very hard being in these casts, depending on other people for everything."

"It won't be too much longer." Maggie didn't know if this was true or not, but she wanted to be reassuring.

To her relief, Candy smiled. "As soon as I get the walking casts, I'll be going home."

"Well, you take care now."

Maggie wished Anna had chosen her words more carefully. But Candy seemed to appreciate this acknowledgement of her worries.

"Thank you, Anna. I'll try." She swiped at her eyes once more, and offered a wavering smile. "Now that I know about the Angel of Death," she added in a whisper, "I'm being very watchful."

4

The Bee women were somber as they gathered at the van. They were still stunned, not only with Candy's paranoia, but with her hysterical treatment of Louise. Before they left her room, Victoria, in her gentle way, had suggested she call Louise so Candy could say goodbye to her. Candy's color had immediately risen, and she'd adamantly refused.

"That Louise always thinks she knows everything. Well, this time she's wrong." Candy's mouth was set in a thin, firm line. "I'll see her again when she wants to apologize."

Maggie and Victoria held a quick conference outside the door and decided it would be better if Louise came another day and worked it out with Candy. Candy was just too upset at the moment—probably a combination of her accident, her friend's death, and her desire to return to her own home. Neither mentioned her paranoia, though it figured largely in their decision.

Grim expressions were the norm as they gathered outside the care center. Candy's attitude was affecting more than just Louise, who was distressed at not resolving their differences. Clare and Edie were unusually quiet. Anna looked ready to cry.

Maggie stifled a sigh. Even the sweet smell of freshly mown grass couldn't overcome the troubled feeling in Maggie's heart left by Candy's story. Nor the sight of the lovely garden.

Victoria too was looking at the garden. "It's a lovely facility," she said. "I can't believe there's any truth to Candy's ideas."

"Yes, I think it's a very nice place," Maggie said. Her eyes returned to the greenery opposite the parking lot. "Such a beautiful garden. Candy didn't say whether or not she got to go outside."

"I guess it's okay—for a place like this," Edie conceded. "But she may not be so far off with her ideas about that Angel of Death. I just read an article in the paper about some therapist killing patients in a nursing home. An inhalation therapist, I think he was. It happens more than people think. The facilities try to hush it up." She ended with a decisive nod. "Bad for business."

Maggie felt relieved that Edie had waited until now to mention this. Candy certainly didn't need any more ammunition supporting her strange idea. But Maggie wasn't in the mood to hear more about caregivers playing god. Thankfully, Louise stepped in.

"Nevertheless, Edie, as Candy herself said, in those cases you hear about in the papers—and the one she mentioned from television—the patients who are killed are very, very ill. Terminally ill, in most cases. The so-called Angels, however misguided, feel that they're helping the patients by easing them out of their pain. Or giving them the dignity of a peaceful death when their lives might have been artificially prolonged. Candy isn't ill. She's just recovering from her broken legs. She'll be fine in no time at all, and go on home. Then she'll probably laugh about her fears."

As Louise finished speaking, they stepped away from the building, and the brooding appearance of the sky became apparent. So recently blue, the sky was rapidly darkening, the edge of the horizon blurred with thick reddish-brown clouds.

"Oh, dear."

Maggie wasn't sure who said it, but it was the perfect comment. Six heads tipped upward, then turned as one toward the horizon. The mountains that should have been visible there were gone. The red-brown cloud that concealed them was growing every second and visibly moving toward them.

"My mother always said a sky that color meant something terrible was going to happen," Edie informed them.

After the disturbing visit with Candy, that was the last thing Maggie wanted to hear. And she could see that Edie's comment disturbed both Anna and Clare. "It's just a dust storm, Edie. You're letting Candy's paranoia color your thinking."

Louise hurried toward her van. "I think we'll be back at the church before it hits. We don't have far to go."

Louise's voice was calm, but Maggie recognized the set of her chin. It seemed Edie's foreboding of doom had affected more than just Clare and Anna. Maggie herself had to admit to an unfocused dread spreading through her midsection.

"This is an odd time of year for a big dust storm," Edie insisted, as they climbed into the van. "It's much too early for monsoon weather."

"Nevertheless, we seem to be experiencing it," Louise said, turning the key with a quick movement of her wrist. The engine caught immediately and Louise lost no time in backing from the space.

Maggie sensed that Louise was holding on to her temper with difficulty. The unexpected conflict with Candy had surely upset her, and now to have to cope with Edie's predictions of gloom. Was paranoia catching?

"No one can ever predict the weather accurately," Victoria observed. "And it was hotter than normal today."

Maggie was grateful for Victoria's calm, decisive comments. Her serene outlook was just what was needed at the moment. And a change of topic wouldn't hurt either.

"What did you do while you waited for us, Louise?"

"I looked around, and talked to a few people." While she spoke, Louise kept a wary eye on the rearview mirror and the approaching storm. "Candy may not be happy there, but everyone I spoke to was."

"Did you go into other rooms?" Clare asked.

"No. There's a large day room just down the hall from Candy's room. It's very nice—bright and sunny with a lovely quilt hanging on the wall. There were several people in there who seemed to enjoy visiting with me."

"Candy really thinks there's an Angel of Death working there."

Anna's voice showed her apprehension. Maggie thought she half believed Candy, even though she didn't want to.

"Yes." Clare picked up from Anna. "She claims she heard him creeping about outside her room last night."

Maggie sighed. "Her theory is that the care center personnel would be rushing about, not moving in such a quiet manner."

"Oh, I don't know." Louise replied to the unspoken question. "Late at night, I think they would try to be quiet, try not to wake the patients."

Louise pulled into the church parking lot—still ahead of the storm. The others breathed an audible sigh of relief. But Maggie did not. The eminent storm was far from her mind.

For while she didn't want to linger on Candy's certainty that someone was killing people in the care center, her friend's paranoia continued to bother Maggie.

5

For all of her married life, Maggie had lived on a ranch in the mountains north of Scottsdale. When she and her husband settled there after their wedding, the area was an unincorporated part of Maricopa County. But in recent years most of the northern valley had been claimed by either Phoenix or Scottsdale, and the ranch became part of the booming North Scottsdale area. When her beloved Harry died, Maggie left the ranch in the care of her eldest son, Hal, and moved to a condominium near downtown Scottsdale.

But some traditions continued. Every Sunday, the family attended mass at St. Rose then gathered at the ranch for brunch. Not everyone made it every week. Maggie was always there, and Hal's family, of course—his wife Sara and their two sons. Maggie had three other sons. Frank was a veterinarian, married with a young daughter. Bobby and his wife, both teachers, were expecting their first child soon.

And then there was Michael. Her baby. He might be a big strapping police officer, but he was still her baby. He was the one who most often missed the Sunday brunches because of his varying work schedule. So Maggie had him over for dinner every Monday night, whenever his schedule allowed. He made it more often than not.

On this Monday, Maggie was glad that she had already

done much of the dinner preparations. The dark sky they'd seen on leaving the care center had indeed been a prediction of gloom. A literal one. The dust storm hit just as they returned to St. Rose to claim their cars and go home, immersing the area in an early twilight. With the swirling dust reducing visibility to a few feet, the women hurried inside to wait out the storm.

The extra hour of stitching they achieved gave them a chance to discuss Candy's paranoia. But they couldn't reach any conclusions since they lacked the necessary knowledge of her condition and medications.

When the storm cleared enough for the women to feel comfortable driving, Maggie discovered that the unexpected storm had snarled traffic. She made it home just in time to put the already prepared meatloaf into the oven and start the potatoes and vegetables. It would be an old-fashioned meal tonight, but one that she knew Michael would enjoy.

As it was, Maggie needn't have worried about the timing of her meal. Michael was late.

"Sorry I'm late, Ma." Michael leaned over to kiss Maggie's cheek. "Lot of rush hour accidents today."

Maggie nodded. "The weather, of course."

He agreed. "Thought I'd never finish up the paperwork."

He followed his mother as she hurried back to the kitchen, sniffing with pleasure. "Mmm. Meatloaf."

Maggie smiled. Nothing like an appreciative diner. "With mashed potatoes."

"And gravy?"

Maggie stopped in front of the oven, mitts in hand, and raised an eyebrow. "Is there any other way?"

Within minutes they were seated at the table, Michael

digging into the meal with enthusiasm.

"So, tell me about your visit with Judy."

Two months before, Michael met an actress touring with *The Phantom of the Opera*. He'd just returned from a short visit to Denver, the tour's current stop, to visit her.

Maggie was glad to see the smile that appeared at the mention of Judy's name. Maggie liked the young woman with the operatic voice.

"She's great. She said to be sure and say hello. And to tell you that she's doing well with the piecing."

During the play's run in the valley, Maggie gave Judy a few quilting lessons. Judy's grandmother had been a quilter and she was delighted to have the opportunity to learn hand piecing.

It was Maggie's turn to smile. "I knew the Grandmother's Flower Garden was just the thing for her."

At Michael's blank look, Maggie sighed. "Honestly, you boys just never pay attention to the quilt patterns."

Michael's grin was enough to charm a frown off a statue. His mother could never resist it.

"I guess that must be the name of that quilt she's making, huh? All those hexagons that look like flowers?"

Maggie's mouth turned down at one corner as she scolded her son. "You naughty boy. You knew all along didn't you?"

He laughed. "She showed me what she's done and I recognized it. You used to have a quilt like that on the guest room bed."

"Well, I guess you earn points for observation."

"Hey, I'm a cop. I've got powers of observation most people only hope for."

Another grin.

Maggie finished her meal and folded her hands across

41

the table in front of her. Michael was helping himself to seconds of everything. She did like to see her boys with healthy appetites.

"We went out to the Palo Verde Care Center today to see Candy Breckner."

Maggie didn't have to tell Michael she meant the Quilting Bee. He would know whom she meant by "we." Michael called them her "gang."

"How is she? That was a terrible accident."

Maggie frowned while she considered her answer.

Michael, mopping up the last of the gravy with a biscuit, looked up from his meal. He watched his mother as he chewed the last bite.

"That bad?"

"No, no. It's not that. She's not really sick, you know, just recovering. She can't manage on her own until her legs are healed, and she's frustrated at being in the care center and dependent on others for everything." Maggie piled the dirty plates in front of her, reaching for Michael's to add to the stack. "It's just that she told us a disturbing story. And I'd like to get your opinion."

Michael raised an eyebrow but refrained from commenting.

Maggie stood, taking the stacked plates over to the sink and placing them on the counter. "Let me cut you a piece of cake and I'll tell you about it while you eat."

Maggie brought the dessert plates and forks over to the table before removing the cover from the cake keeper. A fuzzy white cake graced the platter beneath.

"Coconut cake!"

Michael's delight made Maggie smile. She hadn't made a coconut cake in a long time. It had long been a childhood favorite of Michael and his friend Jonathan, who had been murdered earlier in the year. Memories of that young life lost had haunted Maggie, but she'd decided it was past time to put it behind her. Making the cake was another step forward.

Once they were settled, Michael with a thick slice in front of him, Maggie with a sliver on the plate before her, Maggie began to tell Michael about Candy. Maggie's dessert lay ignored while she explained about Candy's tale of unusual deaths, the television show she'd seen, and her suspicions.

"Michael, she's convinced that someone is out to kill her. Do you think there's any possibility at all that there's a homicidal maniac there?"

"Homicidal maniac?" Michael raised an eyebrow. "Ma. Listen to yourself."

Maggie had to smile. A new perspective helped a lot. "I guess you're right. I do sound slightly demented myself talking that way." Maggie sighed. "It just bothers me. Candy has always been a very practical person. And she's not very imaginative. She doesn't even create her own embroidery or quilt designs, just follows patterns in books. I don't know what's come over her."

"Did she hit her head in the accident? A head injury can have strange side effects."

Maggie pursed her lips while she considered this.

"I don't think so. I don't remember her mentioning it, and she doesn't have any noticeable bruises. Except for what was probably caused by the airbag."

"What about medication? Drugs, even common ones, can really do a job on some people."

"That's a possibility. I thought of that myself. She's probably on some kind of pain medication, don't you think?"

Maggie thought this over while she finally savored a bite of her cake. "That would explain some other things too. She seems to think her daughter is more interested in her business than in her, and she told us her son-in-law and her two stepchildren don't care about her or what happens to her. And she got so rattled at Louise this afternoon!"

She went on to tell him about Louise trying to make Candy admit she had nothing to worry about, and Candy's over-reaction. "She actually shouted at her to get out of the room, Michael." Maggie shook her head. "It was terrible."

"Was this unusual behavior too, or did she always have a temper?"

"Candy's always been emotional. But as to a temper . . ." Maggie shrugged. "Sometimes I guess. She can get all riled up about something, but then she gets over it quickly, and apologizes. Today was different. Before we left, Victoria suggested she call in Louise so Candy could say goodbye. And she got all upset again. All red in the face. She looked so upset that we thought it best if Louise didn't go back in to see her today."

"Well, if her personality has changed, then it's sure to be a problem with medication. That's what happens with drug addicts."

Michael finished his slice of cake and looked so disappointed to see it gone, Maggie hopped back up to get him another piece. Once they were settled back at the table, Maggie with a fresh cup of coffee, they returned to their interrupted conversation.

"I wouldn't worry about her, Ma. If it is a drug problem, the staff will notice and make an adjustment. And as for this Angel of Death thing . . . A lot of people see something like that on television, or read about it in the newspaper and imagine it's happening to them. It's not uncommon. We get calls all the time from people who think something they heard about on TV is happening to them."

Michael took a long drink of milk, eying his mother warily. "Now, don't take this the wrong way, Ma, but calls like that come especially from older women who live alone."

Maggie's eyes sparked, but she remained silent. She knew what he said was true.

"It's part loneliness, part fear," Michael continued. He took up his fork to finish the last of the cake. "If you're concerned about her, you could ask one of the nurses or doctors out there. Or talk to her daughter about it. That's Andrea Radford's mother, isn't it?"

Maggie nodded.

"She went to school with Bobby, remember?"

"Hmm, I didn't." Maggie's mouth curved into a wry smile. "The memory is the first thing to go, you know."

Michael threw back his head and laughed. "Nothing's going on you, Ma. You're sharp as a tack, and you know it."

6

Maggie picked up Victoria for the ride to St. Rose's the next morning. Many of the Senior Guild members attended morning mass to begin their day, but Maggie had not gotten into the habit. When she lived on the ranch, she was too far out to make the trip each morning; once she'd moved into town, she met Victoria and began carpooling. Victoria was a Lutheran, whom Maggie met at a condominium complex function. Quickly finding many interests in common, they became instant friends; it wasn't long before Maggie had introduced Victoria to the Quilting Bee. They had been friends for years now, and knew each other very well. So when Victoria got into the car and leaned her head against the headrest, Maggie gave her a penetrating look.

Victoria looked exhausted. Maggie also noted that Victoria wore makeup this morning. A stylish dresser, and always careful of her appearance, Victoria nevertheless usually saved makeup base for dressier occasions. Lipstick and blush were usually enough for Bee mornings.

Not that the use of makeup this morning could hide its purpose from Maggie. Even through the concealer and base, Maggie could see the dark circles underscoring her friend's eyes. She'd bet the old ranch that Victoria hadn't slept much the night before. And since her own sleep had been troubled by restless dreams, she suspected she knew the reason behind Victoria's problem. But it was a short ride to St. Rose. If Maggie wanted to learn anything specific about Victoria's sleepless night, she'd have to ask now.

"So how was your evening?"

Maggie kept her eyes on the road as she eased out of their complex and onto the street, but she heard a sigh come from the passenger side of the car.

"I had a very restless night," Victoria admitted.

Maggie could hear the smile in Victoria's voice at her next words.

"You noticed the makeup, didn't you? I should have known I couldn't fool you." She sighed again. "But I looked so pale . . ."

"Do you feel all right?"

"Oh, yes." Quickly. Reassuring. "I just couldn't stop thinking about Candy."

Ahh, Maggie thought. Softhearted Victoria.

"I lay in my nice comfortable bed, and I felt warm and safe. And I just couldn't stop thinking of Candy there, in that strange place, probably also lying awake, but badly frightened, staring at the door and listening for strange footsteps."

It was Maggie's turn to sigh. "Candy never struck me as the fanciful sort. She doesn't even come up with her own quilt or embroidery patterns. I was surprised at that story of hers. Do you think she hit her head in the accident? A head injury might explain it."

"I don't know. I don't recall hearing anything about a head injury."

Victoria paused. Maggie assumed she was picturing the woman they had seen yesterday.

"She didn't have any bad bruises—just the ones from the

airbag. But I suppose she could have an injury that's hidden in her hair."

Victoria twisted in her seat so that she could look at Maggie. "At around two o'clock this morning, I had an idea. What if Candy had a new quilt project to occupy her time? Maybe she wouldn't dwell on these strange suspicions then."

Maggie considered this for a moment, then nodded. "It's an idea. What did you have in mind?"

"Well, I thought I might cut some patchwork squares and take them out to her. She likes to do handwork, and she didn't seem especially interested in the needlepoint pillow she's working on now."

Maggie nodded her agreement just as she turned into the parking lot at St. Rose. "It's a wonderful idea. I'll help you organize something."

"Let's tell the others." For the first time that morning, Victoria offered a genuine smile. "Maybe they'll contribute some fabric squares as well."

Victoria's step seemed lighter as she headed for the Bee room, with Maggie dragging behind her. The other women readily agreed when Victoria described her idea to help Candy. They would all bring four-inch fabric squares the next day; they were large enough for Candy to work on easily, and progress would be rapid. Everyone hoped it would cheer her to see results quickly.

"I'm so glad you all like my idea," Victoria said. "I'll take the fabric out to Candy tomorrow, after our meeting."

"I have a straw basket I can bring," Louise told them. "I'll line it with fabric to make it pretty and we can put everything in it. She can set it on the table beside her to keep everything together."

"I'll put in a needlebook," Edie offered. "I make them

for gifts and usually have a few on hand. We can fill it with threaded needles. She might be on pain medication—sometimes that can affect your eyesight."

Edie surprised Maggie with such a sensible suggestion. Everyone complimented Edie for the proposal.

Clare also had an idea. "We should offer to pick up whatever she sews in a day or two and press them out. She won't be able to do the pressing there, and the blocks look so much better after they're pressed."

Everyone agreed that was an excellent plan.

Anna smiled. "We'll take turns, that way she'll have lots of company too."

No one mentioned it, but Maggie knew they were all thinking along the same lines—that more visitors might also help her stop imaging killer nurses with filled hypodermics roaming the halls of the care center.

Louise, however, looked troubled. "Perhaps I shouldn't go."

"I'm sure Candy will have forgotten all about it by now," Victoria assured her.

But Maggie wasn't so sure. "She does usually get over a temper quickly," she said. "If that's all it was. I talked with Michael last night and he mentioned that medication could cause a change in personality."

Louise nodded. "It can. It could also explain her theory of a killer nurse."

"Did Michael have any ideas about the Angel of Death?" Clare wanted to know.

Maggie had to grin. "He thought it was her imagination, of course. He said people often imagine something they see on television is actually happening to them."

"That happens all the time with diseases, too," Louise said. "Someone reads about an illness, or hears a friend describe particular symptoms. And they're sure they have it too. Doesn't matter if it's a disease that is caused by some rare insect bite in sub-tropical Africa. They don't even hear that part. Just the bits about achy joints, or a rash, or whatever."

"I'm sure if you go in with some of the quilt blocks in a day or two, Candy won't even remember that you two quarreled."

Maggie would come to reflect on these words in later days, and wish that no one else had remembered the quarrel either.

7

Since it had been her idea, Victoria made the first visit to Candy the following afternoon. Basket of supplies held firmly in her hands, she and Maggie walked down the hall to Candy's room. A raised voice caused them to hesitate outside the door.

"Take me home. I've been practicing with the crutches. I'll be able to manage."

Even from outside the closed door, Maggie and Victoria could tell that Candy was crying. Her voice wavered and she sounded more like a two year old on the verge of a tantrum than a grown woman in her sixties.

"I can't." The other woman's voice was firm but tired. Young. "You know that Alan and I need time to ourselves. It's hard enough with just the kids. He knows you've never liked him, and our marriage doesn't need that kind of stress right now."

Maggie and Victoria exchanged a glance. They didn't know what to do now. If they walked in, it would be embarrassing for everyone.

The young woman's voice went on. "Besides, I don't care how much you've been practicing, you can't manage on your own right now. And I can't take care of you. I have to be at the store during the day. And you'd be dangerous on crutches with the twins running around—to both them

51

and yourself. When you get back to where you can do things yourself, without crutches, we'll work something out. When the doctor says you can manage on your own again."

Candy replied, but her voice had dropped to more normal levels and they could no longer make out what she was saying. The younger woman's voice, however, carried clearly.

"I have to work. I've put a lot into my business, and I have to be there. It's especially important right now."

This time they heard Candy.

"But I can't stay here. I'm so frightened. He'll kill me, I know it."

"Don't be silly. No one is killing people."

The voices inside stopped. Or became too low for them to hear.

Maggie raised her arm and knocked lightly on the door. If Andrea was getting ready to leave, it wouldn't do for her to find them standing outside as though they were eavesdropping.

Although Maggie had already begun to push the door open, the younger of the two voices called out.

"Come in."

Candy was seated in a wheelchair beside the large window, the Bee's nine-patch friendship quilt covering her lap. She held a fistful of tissues, some of which she used to dab at her face. Standing beside her was a young woman of medium height. Although her hair was now a uniform gray, Maggie knew that Candy had been a true blonde, as was the younger woman. She also shared Candy's nose and eyes. Her mouth, though, was more generous and looked as though it was made for laughter.

But she wasn't laughing now. Her lips were drawn into a smile as she faced the women, but it was obvious to Maggie that she was forcing it. She was trying hard to be polite, but Maggie could see the strain in the lines of her face and the stiffness of her neck.

"Maggie. Victoria." Candy's voice cracked as she greeted them, still quavering from her recent sobbing. "How nice of you to come."

Candy did seem glad to see them, but she too was struggling to find a smile. Her lips quivered as she attempted to lift the corners, then finally settled into a crooked line that would have passed for a smirk if the circumstances had been different—and the look in her eyes less tragic.

Victoria, sensing a need, rushed forward, placing the gift basket on the bed, and gave Candy a hug.

"Candy," Victoria said, as she released Candy and stepped back, "you look well." She turned to the well-dressed young woman, still standing stiffly near the bed. "And you must be Andrea. I've heard so much about you." She offered her hand and Andrea took it.

Maggie noted the short, professional handshake. Andrea had turned into the consummate businesswoman. If she hadn't known it from the clothes, that handshake with its brief moment of eye contact would have cinched it.

Andrea nodded briefly at Maggie, her polite smile still firmly in place. "Mrs. Browne. Nice to see you again."

Andrea picked up a briefcase that sat beside her mother's chair. "Well Mother, since your friends are here to visit, I'll be going. I'm late as it is, but I didn't want to leave you alone just now."

Maggie wanted to roll her eyes, but managed to contain the childish impulse. And people thought *mothers* were the ones who produced guilt in daughters!

Andrea leaned over and kissed her mother's cheek. Maggie noticed the way Candy leaned into it, almost forcing a hug as well. Still reluctant to let her daughter escape, Maggie supposed. Candy was hurting and not quite herself, Maggie tried to remember. Otherwise her mouth might get the best of her, and she might tell Candy a thing or two about independence and common sense. And probably end up in the doghouse along with Louise. Maggie pulled her lips into a tight line as she fought the urge to remonstrate with the other woman.

Candy's eyes remained fixed on her daughter's back until she disappeared behind the closing door. Then she turned her attention to Victoria and Maggie, looking from one to the other as though trying to remember who they were.

"Did you have a restful night?"

Victoria's quiet question broke the silence, but Maggie wished she had found another topic. Didn't she realize that her question was sure to revisit the topic of that restless "angel" Candy had told them about?

Candy sighed, the heavy breath ending with a hiccup of a sob. She raised the wad of tissues to her mouth.

"I slept a little," she told them. "It's not easy sleeping in a strange bed."

Once again Maggie pulled her lips tight, this time pinching them between her teeth for a second. Candy had been in the hospital for a few days, then in the care home for almost a week. While Maggie could understand someone not sleeping well the first, or even second night in a strange bed, Candy should be well past that.

Victoria, however, quietly agreed, going on to tell a story about a two week stay with an aunt when she barely slept a wink because of the lumpy old bed in the guest room.

Candy smiled at Victoria's story.

With their friend in a happier mood, Maggie took the

basket from the bed and pulled a chair up beside Candy's. Victoria followed suit.

"We brought you a little present," Maggie began. "It was Victoria's idea."

"We all helped put it together," Victoria stated firmly.

Candy was looking at the basket in confusion. "You brought me a basket of fabric scraps?"

"It's kind of a quilt in a basket," Maggie suggested.

Victoria nodded. "I thought that you might enjoy having some hand piecing. So we all contributed some four-inch squares for a scrap quilt. They're grouped into sets for four-patch blocks." Victoria picked up a set of four fabric squares to show Candy. There were two light fabrics—a small floral print on a pale pink ground—and two dark. The dark fabric was a deep blue sprinkled with tiny stars.

Maggie took what looked like a small fabric book from the basket. "And in here, we have some needles for you, all pre-threaded." As she spoke, she fanned open the little book, revealing pale wool "pages" pinned with needles. Thread was neatly looped into a circle that sat between the pages, keeping it from snarling.

"It's a medium gray thread," Victoria said, "so that you can use them on any fabric and not have to worry about matching colors."

Maggie put the needlebook back in the basket. "There are scissors and a spool of thread, too. The pre-threaded needles are for when you're feeling tired. It's so hard to thread a needle then, don't you think?"

Candy seemed stunned by the gift basket. Her lips moved but no words emerged.

Maggie and Victoria exchanged a smile. They could see that Candy was thrilled with their gift.

Maggie fingered one of the fabric squares. "We decided

on a four inch block so that it will go together quickly." She smiled at Candy. "There's nothing like seeing results right away."

Victoria reached into the basket, picking out a bright red fabric apple. "Edie made the needlebook and this pin cushion." She held it up, showing that it held several white-headed pins. "We put in everything you need to get going."

Victoria dropped the apple back into the basket, then pulled out the set of fabric squares she'd shown her earlier and handed them to Candy.

"Someone from the Bee will visit in a day or two and pick up the ones you've sewn. We'll press them for you—they look so much nicer when they've been pressed."

Candy, who had arranged the first four squares on her lap, reached for the pincushion, then suddenly stopped. Tears filled her eyes and Maggie doubted she could see what she was doing. One lone tear escaped the outside corner of her eye, rolling over her cheekbone.

"You're so kind to bring me this. It feels good to hold fabric in my hands again." She sniffed, swiping at the tear with one hand. "I've missed it."

Maggie handed her a tissue while Victoria patted her hand. "We're glad to do it," Victoria assured her. "Only another quilter understands how hard it is not being able to sew."

"This will help," Candy assured them.

"Help?" Victoria's face reflected her puzzlement.

"To take my mind off that man," Candy said, her voice lowered almost to a whisper by the last word. She was lining up the first two squares, setting the pins in carefully. "Hand work always helps me relax."

Maggie could already see the difference in Candy as she pushed her needle into the fabric. The change in her was amazing. Maggie wanted to inquire about "that man," but she decided to let it go for now. Candy was looking so much more like her normal self. Why upset her again with a reference to the Angel of Death?

8

While Victoria encouraged Candy to sort through the basket, Maggie excused herself. She wanted to look around, see the layout of the facility, perhaps observe some of the employees at work. She wondered if Candy suspected one particular individual of being the Angel of Death, or if she just sensed something sinister.

As Maggie stepped out into the hall, she had to shake her head at her use of the word sinister, even in her thoughts. "Sinister" was the Bates Motel. At the Palo Verde Care Center, the staff moved with purposeful strides through bright, clean halls, smiles ready to greet patients and visitors alike. Framed floral prints decorated the mint green walls, and an ivy border had been stenciled just below the ceiling. "Cheerful" seemed much more appropriate.

A few steps from Candy's room, Maggie discovered the community room Louise had described. This room, in fact all of the building that she'd seen on her two visits, was clean, comfortable, and well lit.

Maggie was charmed by the large quilt hanging on one wall: a Log Cabin pattern in forest green, salmon, and lemon yellow. There were fresh flowers on a table, a television where several women were engrossed in a soap opera, and an easy chair where another woman sat crocheting an afghan. Near the sliding doors that led out into the garden, two men sat at a card table playing Scrabble. Another card table held a partially assembled jigsaw puzzle.

"Mrs. Browne? Is that you?"

Maggie turned. A tall redhead in hospital scrubs printed with a bright tropical pattern walked toward her. She didn't look familiar, but Maggie offered a smile anyway. The older she got, the more people she knew, and the harder it was to remember them all.

"You won't remember me. Tara Dillion," she said, offering her hand. "I used to be Tara McClintock. I went to school with Bobby."

Maggie stepped back to better view the young woman, her eyes traveling from her short practical hairstyle to her white tennis shoes. "Tara McClintock. I do remember you." The carrot-red hair had darkened to a beautiful deep auburn, the gangly teenage body filled out into a mature young woman's figure. "You've changed, of course."

Tara laughed. "Oh, goodness, I sure hope so. Still have the freckles though," she added, running her finger across her nose.

Maggie smiled. "And I'll bet your husband thinks they're as cute as can be."

Tara laughed again, agreeing that he did.

For several minutes Maggie spoke of Bobby, catching Tara up on his current life as a middle school teacher.

"I'll bet he's a wonderful teacher. He's such a nice guy and has more patience than any man I know."

Maggie silently agreed. Bobby was the gentlest of her sons, the one who always had time to listen.

"I run into him now and then," Tara told her, "but not recently." Her hand ran softly over her belly. "You'll have to tell him I'm expecting." Her lips tipped into a shy smile. "Our first."

Now that she'd mentioned it, Maggie could detect a slight roundness where Tara's hand pressed against the front of her loose shirt. She smiled as she took hold of the younger woman's hand, offering a squeeze of congratulations. Although Tara was similar to Maggie in height and build, Tara's hands were much larger. It took both of Maggie's slender hands to cover one of Tara's.

Tara quickly reversed the position, covering Maggie's hands with her own. "Your hands are so cold, Mrs. Browne." Tara's voice was filled with concern. "I was on my way to the staff lounge for some coffee. Would you like a cup?"

"Thank you, yes. And do call me Maggie." She rubbed her hands together as they started down the hall. "I hadn't realized how cold they were until I felt the warmth of your hands. It's the air conditioning. I'm always cold indoors once the air conditioning comes on." Maggie pushed both hands into the pockets of her slacks. "Of course, it's better than the alternative. I remember the days before refrigeration, and I sure wouldn't want to do without it again. Especially at my age."

Tara smiled at Maggie's comments, assuring her that she was still young, as she led the way down the hall. "What on earth did you do in the summer before air conditioning?"

"Oh, we had swamp coolers," Maggie began.

"That's right! Our neighbors had one." Tara's exclamation interrupted Maggie as she recounted her memory of the old style coolers. A more primitive design than modern air conditioning, evaporative or swamp coolers operated by blowing air over wet pads. It brought the temperatures down nicely, but only when the humidity was low. "Their house was always cooler than ours in the spring, but it got very warm in August."

Maggie smiled. "That sounds about right. Years ago, it cooled down more at night, too, because the valley wasn't as built up. All that asphalt and concrete holds in the heat."

They'd reached the end of the hall, just before the emergency exit door; Tara opened a door marked "staff only" and ushered Maggie inside.

The staff room was cozy, the walls a pale robin's egg blue. There were no quilts or fresh flowers here, but there was a small refrigerator, a microwave, a coffee maker, and a table lined with chairs. A blue pitcher filled with silk daisies sat on a paper doily at the center of the table. Several travel posters had been tacked to the walls. Along the side wall was a long couch where a young man in blue scrubs was stretched out, apparently napping.

Tara looked at him then rolled her eyes at Maggie. "Joseph."

There was no reaction from the figure on the couch.

Tara stepped closer and raised her voice. "Joseph."

This time the young man came awake with a jolt. He sat straight up, then swung his legs over so that his feet landed flat on the floor.

"I'm up, Tara." He stood and headed for the door, flashing a charming smile at the women as he passed them. "I was just going back out."

"Good. Mr. Branford was looking for you to help him walk outside."

Tara watched him leave, a smile tipping her lips.

"He's a pretty good worker, but I think he likes to party. He sure doesn't seem to get enough sleep at night. All his breaks seem to be spent napping on that couch. If he weren't so charming, he'd be long gone. But the patients all love him." She shook her head. "It's so hard to find good, reliable help."

While Tara poured their coffee, Maggie seated herself at the table. There was no pleasant garden view here. The window in the small lounge looked out at the parking lot.

Tara brought over the coffee, seating herself across from Maggie.

"I hope you don't mind decaf. I drink a lot of coffee and I'm trying to cut back on caffeine now that I'm pregnant."

Maggie assured her it was fine.

Tara sighed. "It's not the same; but I searched long and hard for a really good brand." She took a long sip, closing her eyes with pleasure. When she'd swallowed, she opened her eyes, giving Maggie a sheepish look. "I must be getting used to it. It tastes darn good."

Maggie wrapped her hands around her mug, enjoying the warmth exuding from it. Steam rose from the cup and she was reluctant to sip at it and chance burning her mouth, even though Tara had done it with no apparent ill effect. The aroma drifting upward was heavenly, and making her mouth water.

"So, are you visiting one of my patients?"

Maggie nodded. "I'm here with another friend to see Candy Breckner."

"Mmm. Andrea's mother."

"That's right, she was in school with you and Bobby, wasn't she?"

"Yes. I knew her, but she wasn't part of the crowd I hung around with. I hadn't seen her in years, though I've kept up with her business activities in the newspaper."

"That gift shop of hers is a nice place. Lots of unusual things. But expensive."

"Just what I'd expect from Andrea. Even as a teenager, she had exquisite taste. Always the best clothes, the chicest hair-dos." Tara sighed. "I keep saying I'm going to go and check out her shop, but somehow I'm always too busy. There are never enough hours in the day for all I want to do."

Tara took another sip of her coffee.

"So you and Candy are friends?"

"Yes." Maggie smiled; she was enjoying this visit. "We both belong to the Senior Guild at St. Rose."

"Do you? I belong to St. Rose too." Tara offered Maggie a broad smile. "So you're part of the group that does the Halloween Bazaar?"

Maggie nodded.

"I love the Bazaar! I wish they'd done it when I was a kid."

Maggie's smile widened. "I belong to the St. Rose Quilting Bee. We do the quilts . . ." Tara nodded. "My friend Victoria Farrington—she's in visiting with Candy now—is also in the Quilting Bee. Candy is a sometime member, but we consider her one of us." Maggie's tone was indulgent. "Candy likes variety, so she flutters among the various needlework groups."

Tara looked startled. "It's hard to picture Candy 'fluttering'."

Maggie stopped with her cup halfway to her lips, which turned down at Tara's comment.

"Oh, I don't mean because of her injuries," Tara hastened to explain. "It's just that she can be very stubborn and difficult. She won't let Joseph work with her for instance—you know, the young man who was in here when we arrived?"

Maggie nodded.

"Joseph is very popular with the other patients. He's cheerful and he kids around with them. Tells silly jokes. Flatters the women. But Candy doesn't want him anywhere near her. Practically got hysterical this morning when he tried to help her out of bed."

Maggie finally ventured a taste of the decaf, and it was every bit as good as it smelled. In fact, she'd been ready to compliment Tara on the excellent coffee and inquire as to where she could buy some, when Tara made her comment about Candy. Maggie wondered if she should mention Candy's Angel of Death theory. Would she have told the administration about her fears? Was that why she didn't want Joseph to work with her? Was she leery of all the male employees, or of him in particular?

But while Maggie debated the wisdom of bringing up Candy's paranoia, Tara continued with her complaint.

"I never thought I'd ever say this, but I wish Candy's family wouldn't visit so often."

"Really? Why is that?" Maggie was surprised. She'd always assumed that the nursing staff in these facilities encouraged family to visit.

Tara shook her head. "I'm not sure exactly. But she's always agitated and weepy after they leave. And much harder to deal with."

"Andrea was with her when we arrived. It sounded like they were arguing about her going home. We couldn't help but overhear them. Candy was crying."

"See? That's exactly what I mean." Tara's mouth pulled down into a concerned frown. "She complains about dizzy spells and shortness of breath after they leave, and that's when she gets whiney and demanding. It's even worse after her stepchildren visit. She asks us to check her blood pressure, and sometimes it is up. But I think most of her problems are the result of self-induced stress."

Maggie digested this information while she took another sip of her coffee; again she wondered if she should ask whether Candy had mentioned the Angel of Death. But before she could bring it up, Tara went on.

"And now she's gotten paranoid as well. She tried to tell me someone here is killing people, like a case in California that she saw on television. Insisted on whispering so I could hardly hear what she was saying." Tara's lips turned down in disgust.

Maggie nodded. "She told us about that when we came to visit on Monday. About the television show and how she suspected the same thing was happening here."

Tara emptied her cup and rose to get the carafe from the coffeemaker. She refilled her cup and topped off Maggie's. Although her expression remained neutral, Maggie had the distinct impression that she was counting to ten. This notion was reinforced when Tara returned the carafe to the coffeemaker and sat back down with a heavy sigh.

"I didn't realize she was telling everyone."

Maggie didn't know what to say to that, so she remained silent.

"This is a highly respected care home, Mrs. Browne. Maggie," Tara corrected herself. "And we charge accordingly. I hope no one believes that could happen here." Tara frowned. "It could cause some serious problems for us if people actually believe her."

Maggie was surprised at the sudden coolness in Tara's voice. Of course, Tara probably didn't want to lose her job when she had a baby on the way, so she would be concerned about the facility's reputation.

"Did she mention who it is she thinks is killing people?" Maggie asked.

"No. At least, I don't think so. Like I said, she was whispering and acting paranoid in general . . . I wondered if I should get a psychiatrist in to talk to her." Tara frowned.

"It's not always easy knowing the right thing to do. Her friend Rhonda had died overnight and I think that was much of the problem. She didn't want to accept the fact that Rhonda died. And then she'd just seen that program and it gave her this idea . . ."

Tara took a sip from her mug and met Maggie's eyes as she set it back down. "We have a good staff here, Maggie. And there are checks and balances, as clichéd as that might sound. That kind of thing would never happen here."

Maggie wanted to ask about Jane. And she would have liked more information about Rhonda's general health and cause of death. But after her decisive statement, Tara drained her cup and stood. Maggie, recognizing such obvious body language, stood as well. She thanked Tara for the coffee and politely offered to help clean up. But she knew their conversation was at an end.

9

Candy looked relaxed and cheerful when Maggie returned—at least compared to her condition when they'd first arrived. She'd sewn several of the fabric squares together and showed them off to Maggie, telling her that she might make them into a baby quilt for her new grandchild; her stepson Nathan's wife was pregnant.

Maggie looked at Victoria, a hopeful smile on her lips. "So, Nathan's been over to visit?" Maggie couldn't help but remember Candy saying at their last visit that Nathan and Stephanie didn't care about her at all.

But Candy wasn't reading much into her stepson's visit. "He and his wife came over. He always does the polite thing; I'll give him that. Ken taught him manners."

Victoria intervened, showing Maggie an assortment of fabric squares they had separated from the others in the basket.

"Candy wants nice bright colors for the baby quilt," she said. "A much better idea than the soft pastels so many people use, don't you think?"

Maggie agreed, which brought a smile from Candy. "We'll go through our fabric and tell the others, Candy. Now that we know what you want, I'm sure we'll find lots of bright colors for you."

"Perhaps Louise might bring them," Victoria suggested.

Candy didn't turn red, or shout this time. In fact, she barely nodded at Victoria's words, her eyes intent on the needle and the fabric in her hands.

Maggie and Victoria exchanged a look. Candy seemed to have recovered from her outburst on Monday. Or had she not even heard Victoria's words?

They discussed it as they left the building, deciding that she was probably over it.

"Whatever it was that had her so angry and emotional, I guess it's passed," Victoria said. "Maybe it was due to medication, and it's been taken care of now."

"I hope so," Maggie replied. "Though it hasn't seemed to help where that Angel of Death thing is concerned. I met one of the nurses while I was wandering around—a woman who went to school with Bobby," she added with a smile. "Tara McClintock. Tara Dillion now. A very nice woman she's turned into, too."

Maggie decided to ignore that moment of doubt she'd had when they spoke of the possible effect of Candy's rumors.

"Candy has mentioned the Angel of Death to her, but she didn't name anyone. And Tara doesn't believe any of it, of course."

"Understandable." Victoria opened the door for Maggie. "I stayed away from the whole Angel of Death thing while we were talking. I didn't want to encourage her, though she did mention it."

Victoria frowned, her forehead wrinkling in consternation. Then she shook her head slightly, the skin of her forehead smoothed, and she went on speaking. "What I did do was talk a little about Louise while we were stitching together. She didn't get upset, thankfully. Not that she seemed very happy to talk about Louise, but she didn't turn red and say she didn't want her here. I think she'll be glad to see her tomorrow."

Maggie took a deep breath. Part of it was relief that her two friends would no longer have disagreeable words between them. Part of it was just the opportunity to be outside, out of the unnatural indoor air of the care center. While there was no antiseptic, hospital smell, there was still something stifling about being closed up in a building with so many people needing close personal care. Out here, there might no longer be the sweet scent of freshly mown grass, but there was a clean odor of damp earth that Maggie found appealing. And it felt so blessedly warm after the artificial coolness of the overworked air conditioning!

"It's a nice day for a ride," Maggie announced, taking in another deep breath.

Victoria smiled. "It could be a hundred and ten degrees out and you'd think it was a nice day for a ride."

Maggie didn't argue. "I think I'll head out to the ranch when I get home. It's been a few days since I was out to ride Chestnut." Mention of her beloved mare brought a smile to Maggie's lips.

"Exercise sounds like a good idea." Victoria grinned at Maggie. "But I'll take mine indoors, thank you. I think I'll drop into an exercise class this afternoon. It's been a while since I went."

No dust storms darkened the horizon as Maggie and Victoria climbed into the car. Thankfully, the weather had returned to normal after Monday's unusual storm.

Victoria stopped the car at the end of the driveway, preparing to turn out onto the main road. A comment she started about the increased traffic in Scottsdale stopped in her throat when a large owl swooped out of the old olive tree, dipped over the car, then rose into the sky and flew out of sight. Maggie and Victoria stared at the magnificent bird until it was nothing but a dark speck against the intense blue of the sky.

"I didn't know they came out in the daytime." Victoria's voice was suitably hushed.

"They do sometimes." Maggie's voice was also low. She too had been awed by the sight of the magnificent bird. "The Indians say they're harbingers of doom." Maggie's lips tightened into a grim line. She was remembering the thick reddish hue of the horizon after their last visit, hearing Edie's voice saying it meant disaster was ready to strike.

And now, another ill omen.

As Victoria finally turned onto Indian School Road, Maggie leaned her head against the back of the seat and closed her eyes. If there were any other portents of disaster out there, she didn't want to see them.

10

Despite an enjoyable ride in the late afternoon, and a pleasant dinner with her eldest son's family, Maggie spent a restless night. Dreams of owls swooping out of a red sky and nurses with hypodermic needles skulking through shadowy corridors troubled her sleep. Her eyes were red-rimmed and underscored with dark circles when she entered the Quilting Bee room the next morning. It was Victoria's turn to drive, and thankfully she refrained from commenting on Maggie's condition. In fact, Victoria barely said a word, driving over in a thoughtful silence.

In the Quilting Bee room, Edie was less considerate. As soon as she saw Maggie, Edie spoke up. "Goodness, Maggie, you look terrible. Did you get any sleep last night?"

Maggie fumbled with her handbag as she retrieved her reading glasses—her sewing glasses, really—and put the bag into the closet. She knew everyone was watching her.

"You do look awfully tired," Louise said.

Maggie took her time settling into her chair and choosing a needle and thread. She set her glasses, still in their needlepoint case, to one side. She wouldn't need them until her eyes tired.

"I did have some trouble sleeping last night."

Maggie worked her needle in and out of the quilt sandwich, creating a line of small even stitches that curved into a quilted feather design. But even so early in the day, the row of stitches appeared slightly out of focus. She reached for her glasses. She might still feel young, but her eyes were getting old.

Suppressing a sigh, she adjusted the glasses on her nose and resumed her stitching.

"You saw Candy yesterday," Louise said. She cast a searching look from Maggie to Victoria. "Is she still upset with me?"

"No," Victoria said quickly. "Now don't you worry about it, Louise. I told her you would be coming today, and she said it was fine."

"Oh, that's good." Anna expelled a long breath of relief as she clipped off a thread and reached for the spool. "And did she enjoy getting the squares to piece?"

"Yes, she did." Victoria smiled.

Maggie managed to find a smile as well. "She was feeling down when we arrived, crying even. But she was smiling when we left."

"Crying?" Louise asked. "So she still believes that Angel of Death business?"

Maggie nodded. "She still thinks someone is killing the patients there, yes. Her daughter was visiting when we arrived and we could hear raised voices through the door."

"Could you hear what they were saying?" Clare asked. "Were they arguing?"

"I don't think it was really an argument," Victoria replied.

"Candy was asking to go home," Maggie told them. "Pleading actually."

"Candy always does like to have her own way," Edie said. When the others stared at her, she continued. "You just stop and think for a minute. You'll agree with me then.

It's when other people won't go along with doing things her way that she loses her temper." Edie ended with a decisive nod.

There was a short silence while they all stitched. And considered Edie's words.

After a moment of contemplation, Maggie had to agree that Edie was correct. Candy did often behave like a spoiled child when she worked with the Quilting Bee; especially if things weren't done the way she preferred. That might be the real reason she liked to move about rather than stay with one group all the time, Maggie thought.

Victoria's quiet voice broke into what was turning into a lengthy silence. "She's afraid to stay there because of the Angel of Death."

"She should be careful," Edie said. "You never know what people are going to do nowadays. They see things on the television and in the movies, and get ideas." She pursed her lips in disapproval. "So much violence."

Maggie wondered if Edie realized that her words worked two ways. Young hoodlums might get ideas about crimes from television shows. But Candy and her friend may have imagined something happening at their care home because of the program they watched on TV.

"It was very sad, really." Victoria finished stitching a quarter inch around the inside of one of the white nine-patch squares and moved to the next one. "Her daughter was telling her that she couldn't go home."

"Typical. Kids these days have no respect for their parents."

Maggie could often ignore Edie's comments, but it was difficult to do when there was so much truth in them. However, in the case of Andrea and Candy, Maggie knew it was far from simple. And Louise agreed.

"That may be," Louise told Edie. "But I don't see how someone who works full time could handle having a person with two broken legs around."

"From what little we overheard, I think there might be some problems with her marriage too." Maggie looked to Victoria for confirmation.

Victoria nodded. "Andrea said something about their marriage not needing any more stress." She paused while she checked her stitches. Satisfied, she continued. "It would be difficult to have someone like Candy around in the best of times."

The others agreed. Even Anna, who lived with her daughter, admitted that it could be difficult having two women in the house.

"And Andrea has those twins, too," Victoria reminded them. "They couldn't be more than three or four. Raising twins that age can be a full time occupation."

"They just turned four."

Maggie had to smile. Count on Clare to know.

"She was leaving the family birthday party when she had that accident," Clare continued. "Candy said she wanted Andrea to have the party earlier in the day. She was trying to cut down on her nighttime driving. But Andrea said she had to be at the store all day."

"Humph," Edie muttered. "Inconsiderate."

"Candy introduced us to Andrea." Victoria smiled. "Well, she introduced me. I guess Maggie already knew her."

Maggie nodded. "She went to school with Bobby. But I haven't seen her for years."

"A good-looking girl, and so nicely dressed," Victoria said.

"One of the nurses told me Candy always complains of

not feeling well after one of her children visits." Maggie finished her thread and snipped it off.

Without being asked, Louise handed her the spool of thread. "The stress I suppose. Especially if she's pleading with them to take her home each time they come, and going on about her fears that she's going to die."

Victoria, who had just finished her thread as well, took the spool from Maggie. "Maggie knows the head nurse out there," she said, pulling out a length of thread and cutting it.

Maggie, ready to put her needle back into the quilt, paused. She turned sharp eyes toward Victoria, who smiled.

"Tara is the head nurse there?" Maggie's eyebrows rose. "How did you find that out?"

"I have contacts," Victoria replied. She gave Maggie her usual serene smile. "Ryan Dillion is one of the owners of the Palo Verde Care Center. His family built it some fifteen years ago. That's when Scottsdale closed the Palo Verde elementary school and the family acquired the land. The Dillions are an old valley family and own a lot of land in downtown Phoenix. They must have decided to move into Scottsdale."

"Humph. One of those families with more money than they know what to do with," Edie muttered under her breath.

This time the others did ignore her.

"So how do you know the head nurse?" Clare asked Maggie.

"As I said, I didn't realize she was the head nurse. I ran into her in the hall yesterday when I stepped outside Candy's room. I wanted to see how the other rooms were laid out. As Louise said, the day room is very nice. Has a beautiful Log Cabin quilt hanging on one wall." Maggie readjusted her glasses, which felt as though they were sliding down her nose. "I don't know why Candy doesn't sit there with the others, instead of staying in her room."

"She might be afraid to leave her room because of the Angel of Death," Anna suggested.

Maggie wondered if Anna realized that, like Candy, she had lowered her voice to speak of this probable apparition.

"But if she suspects someone is stalking her, why wouldn't she try to stay with other people?"

"She probably feels safer in her room," Anna said. "It probably seems more like home."

Clare nodded absently at Anna's final remark, but the corners of her eyes creased into fine wrinkles as she smiled at Maggie. "You're investigating aren't you? Looking into Candy's suspicions." Her voice was eager. "Were you checking out the staff? Looking for a suspect?"

"No, of course not." Maggie finished another thread and reached for the scissors. She continued to speak as she cut a length of thread and inserted it into the eye of the needle. Even with her glasses on, it took three tries. "I just thought I'd look around. See if what she told us made any kind of sense."

Clare nodded smugly as she traveled her needle through the quilt layers to get from one completed feather loop to the starting place on the next.

Maggie knotted her thread and sunk the knot into the batting. "Anyway, I was admiring the attractive day room . . . It's right down the hall from Candy's. It would be very convenient for her." Maggie took her first stitches. "I was still in the doorway looking into the day room when someone called my name."

"The head nurse?" Anna asked.

"Well, I didn't know she was the head nurse," Maggie

said. "She was wearing one of those scrub suits they all wear nowadays. In a bright tropical print, like a Hawaiian shirt."

"Humph," was Edie's comment to the latter. "Can't hardly tell who the nurses are any more. Whatever happened to those crisp white uniforms and the nice white caps? You knew who the real nurses were then, and who were just nursing assistants."

"Those white uniforms looked nice, of course," Louise said, "but they required a lot of time and energy—washing, bleaching, starching, pressing. The scrub suits are so much more practical. More comfortable too."

"My Aunt Martha was a nurse," Edie said. "She was so proud of that uniform of hers, and especially of her cap. She always kept them both spotless. Today's young people don't want to take the time to do things like laundry properly," Edie intoned. "I doubt they even know how to use real starch," she added with a sniff. "Just that spray stuff in the aerosol can."

"I find that spray starch very practical," Louise said.

Louise winked across the frame at Maggie, who stifled a giggle. Someone her age should not be giggling, Maggie thought, but she and Louise did enjoy sparring with Edie. And, like Louise, Maggie liked the convenience of spray starch.

"What about the head nurse?" Clare asked.

Edie's comments had taken them far from the original topic, and Maggie knew Clare was still interested in what she was calling an investigation. Which it wasn't. But Clare still wanted details.

"Her name is Tara Dillion," Maggie said, "and she went to school with Bobby—and Andrea too, of course. She recognized me as Bobby's mother and said hello. She was very nice. Invited me to have a cup of coffee with her. Decaf. And excellent coffee too. I got the brand name from her."

"You'll have to tell me what it is." Anna sighed. "I'm not supposed to drink regular coffee but the decaf just isn't very good."

Anna's voice lowered as though she was sharing a weighty secret. Maggie couldn't help remembering Candy imparting her confidences.

"Sometimes I mix it with real coffee," Anna admitted. "Half and half."

Maggie hid her smile. You'd think the woman was confessing to adding a little brandy to her coffee. Across the frame, Louise muffled a cough, but Maggie noted that her eyes were twinkling.

"That's nice about the coffee, and you will have to share the brand, but what did she say about Candy's Angel of Death?" Louise deftly returned the conversation to the original topic. "You did ask her, didn't you?"

"Actually, I didn't. She brought it up herself while we were talking about Candy." Maggie considered the previous day's conversation while she examined her most recent stitches. "It makes more sense now that I know she's in charge. But of course she dismissed the whole Angel of Death thing. She is worried, though, that Candy is telling everyone she knows about it. She's afraid it will reflect badly on the care home. Tarnish their reputation."

Another "humph" came from Edie. "Of course she is. Especially if her husband owns it. I'll bet it's an expensive place, too. But who will want to stay in a facility where people are dying in a suspicious manner?"

"If they are," Maggie qualified.

"It doesn't matter if they are or not," Louise said. "Just the suggestion would be enough to ruin their business. Relatives of those who died there recently might sue. No one would want to check in or send their relatives there. They could very quickly go bankrupt." Louise pulled the short length of thread through the cloth and snipped it with a decisive click at the end of her sentence.

"That's a good point," Maggie said. "But the thing that really interested me was her saying that Candy is always in worse shape after a visit from her daughter or stepchildren. She said Candy is difficult after visits. And she complains of things like dizziness and shortness of breath. Things that could be heart problems, but Tara thinks are more like panic attacks. Self-induced stress, I believe she called it."

"I'm not surprised, after what you said earlier," Louise said. "If she's pressing them to take her home every time they visit, and arguing and crying about it, she's probably making herself ill. Her blood pressure might be going up, too—that could make her dizzy, for one thing."

They spent a few minutes discussing various symptoms and what they could indicate. But all agreed that Candy appeared in fine health during their recent visit.

"There was something else Tara said that I found interesting," Maggie told them. "It seems there is a worker there, a young man named Joseph, who Candy dislikes. Tara said she doesn't want him around her, even though the other patients all like him very much. She said Candy got hysterical the other day when he tried to help her out of bed."

Clare's eyes widened and her hands stilled. "Is that who she thinks is the Angel of Death?"

Maggie shrugged. "I don't know. She didn't mention a name to Tara. Or, if she did, Tara didn't mention it."

"Candy told me who she suspects is the Angel of Death."

Victoria's quiet voice stunned the others to silence.

11

Everyone stopped sewing to stare at Victoria, who continued to stitch as though she had just commented on the weather.

Maggie stopped her needle half in and half out of the fabric. "And you didn't tell me yesterday?"

Maggie hoped the hurt she felt didn't come through in her voice. She and Victoria were good friends and usually shared their news. How could Victoria have kept this from her? And the fact that Tara was the head nurse? Of course she might not have known that yesterday afternoon, but surely she could have told her on the drive in this morning.

Maggie realized that Victoria's silence on their short drive that morning had nothing to do with her tactfulness over Maggie's poor appearance. It was now apparent that Victoria had had a lot on her mind.

"I'm sorry, Maggie." Victoria finally did slow her stitching. She looked truly apologetic. "It was such a strange suggestion, I wanted to think it over. And you looked so exhausted after our visit yesterday—with the owl and all."

Mention of an owl so intrigued the other women that Victoria had to stop a moment while she and Maggie described what they had seen. The Angel of Death suspect was temporarily pushed aside by the strange tale of the swooping owl.

There were more predictions of gloom from Edie. She too was familiar with the Indian portent.

Maggie finally took command. She wanted to get Victoria back to Candy's naming of the culprit. She couldn't believe the others weren't as anxious as she was to hear who the suspected miscreant might be.

"So tell us who Candy named as her Angel of Death, Victoria."

Victoria shook her head slowly, a sad smile on her lips. "Poor Candy, I'm worried about how her pain medication may be affecting her mind. She must be on pain medication, don't you think?" She looked around at the others. "I did consider her suggestion quite carefully, and it's still too strange to make any sense."

"But what did she say?"

Maggie silently blessed Clare for saying what she wanted to shout.

"Candy talked to me about it while we were sorting through the fabrics in the basket yesterday. While Maggie was out having coffee with Tara." Victoria drew a deep breath. "She told me she thinks it's the gardener."

"The gardener?" Anna repeated.

Maggie, Louise and Clare just stared at Victoria.

Edie seemed the only one willing to accept the gardener as the culprit. She was nodding. "Gardeners have a lot of opportunity to break into homes. They're around all the time, in closed-in backyards. People barely even see them, because they're like part of the landscape."

Clare, ever ready to consider interesting solutions to a mystery, mulled this over. "Would the gardener have access to the inside of the building?"

"Didn't the deaths occur at night?" Louise asked. "Not exactly the time you'd expect to see the gardener hanging around. Especially indoors."

Victoria shrugged. "I don't know about access, but I'm sure Candy did tell us originally that her friends died overnight. I did find her choice of the gardener troubling. As I said, that's why I didn't say anything to Maggie yesterday. I don't know how she could imagine that the home's gardener could get inside, and in the evening in most cases, and then administer some drug or whatever to kill the patients. And not be discovered."

"Not to mention doing it in a way that makes the professionals there think they were natural deaths," Maggie added.

Clare was thoughtful. "Of course, he could have used a pillow to smother them. That would be easy since most of them are elderly and not in the best of health."

Maggie stared at Clare. The others had also stopped stitching momentarily to look at their colleague.

Maggie felt a chill run down her spine. Their discussion hadn't seemed real somehow until Clare's remark brought home to her how simple it could be to kill one of the care home's frail patients.

Suddenly realizing the effect her words had on the others, Clare flushed pink, bowed her head, and resumed her stitching. "I read a book like that once."

The laughter that followed her remark released the tension around the quilting frame. They all remembered Clare's theories about Jonathan Hunter's murder a few months ago, all found in various mystery books. Clare had a book plot to offer for every suggestion on what might have happened.

Flustered by the laughter, but smiling herself, Clare

went on. "Well, in the book, the killer wasn't the gardener," she said. "It was the cook. Only he wasn't really a cook."

Seeing the perplexed looks on her friends' faces, Clare tried to explain.

"It was in a nursing home, and the character felt the doctor in charge was responsible for killing his wife. So he took a job as the nursing home's cook so he could get his revenge on the doctor. He would sneak into their rooms and smother the patients. And everyone thought it was the doctor doing it. As mercy killings."

"Well, maybe blaming the gardener isn't such a strange theory after all." Victoria was somber.

As were the others. The chill that so recently raced down Maggie's spine was chased by a shudder. Would it really be so difficult to do what Clare described?

"Come, come." Louise chided them out of their gloom, much as she had tried to do with Candy during their fateful visit. This group, however, did not take exception to her opinion. "It was just a book. Maybe Candy read the same book."

Agreeing with this possibility, the others perked up. Maggie, however, still felt a premonition of doom. Was it the owl? Tales heard as a child could affect you in adulthood, even if illogical. That was how old superstitions lived on, why so many people threw salt over their shoulders after spilling some, or avoided black cats and ladders.

With a sigh, Maggie plunged her needle into the fabric. As she brought it back up through the quilt layers, she said a quick prayer for Candy's rapid recovery. The sooner Candy got out of that care center, the better they would all feel.

"Tell them about the baby quilt Candy wants to make."

Maggie thought her voice sounded falsely hearty, but the

others didn't seem to notice. Maggie wanted to believe that Candy's suspicions were unfounded, but this latest example of Clare's didn't help. Neither did the recent unusual weather conditions, and owls swooping out of trees in broad daylight.

Victoria, bless her, picked up the story of Candy and the gift basket. There was nothing like the thought of a baby quilt to cheer a group of quilters, Maggie thought.

"Candy was so excited by our gift," Victoria told them. "She said she really misses her quilting. She asked me to thank all of you for your contributions to the basket."

Victoria let her eyes roam over the other quilters, her lips tipped in a soft smile, her fingers momentarily stationary on the quilt top.

"She decided right away that she would make up the blocks for a baby quilt. Her stepson's wife, Dawn, is expecting a baby in September."

"Nathan's wife," Anna mused. "I'm not sure I know her. Do they come to mass here?"

"Oh, no," Clare told her. "Candy said that Nathan hardly ever went to church. It worried his father. And his wife isn't a Catholic, though she did have their daughter baptized."

"Goodness, Clare, how do you know all this?" Louise asked.

Clare ducked her head, suddenly intent on her next stitch. "Oh, I just enjoy visiting with people. I listen to what they have to say."

And remember it, Maggie thought. And Clare was usually accurate, she had to give her that.

"Anyway," Victoria went on, once again stitching busily on a feather, "Candy and I sorted through the fabrics in the basket and chose the ones that would look nice for a baby quilt. She wanted bright crayon colors. We found quite a few nice combinations, and I told her that I would ask all of you for more."

"I'll run over this afternoon," Louise said. Her eyes troubled, she looked over to Victoria. "You did say that you told her to expect me."

Victoria nodded. "Yes, and she said 'fine.' "

Louise smiled with relief. "Good. It's bothered me that I didn't try to go in and see her again before we left on Monday."

"She was in such a strange mood then, I don't think anything would have been resolved," Maggie told her. "But now . . . Well, she just seems more like her old self."

Louise smiled. "I'll run home before I go and cut some blocks in nice bright colors. And I can pick up the ones she's sewn to iron. Do you think she'll have many done?"

"Oh, yes." Victoria's nod was definite. "She was so happy to be sewing again. She started right in and did several while I was there. It doesn't take long to stitch a four-patch block. I guess I should have brought them with me to press, but she was so proud of what she'd done. I think she wanted to show off the finished blocks to some of the other patients."

"And anyway, I'm sure she'll enjoy the company," Anna said. "Even if she hasn't done more than those few."

Louise didn't seem as certain as Anna did. "I hope so," she murmured. But her voice strengthened as she looked over with a question. "Would you like to come with me, Anna?"

"Oh, dear. I would love to, but the kids have a short day at school today." Anna's voice was genuinely regretful. "And I don't like them to come back to an empty house."

Edie nodded emphatically. "Never know what can

happen. There might be some suspicious characters in the neighborhood. Gardeners, even."

The others looked up briefly, checking to see if Edie was making a joke. But Edie was starting a new thread, concentrating on sinking the knot and beginning her line of stitches. She appeared perfectly serious.

"Your daughter is lucky to have you there," Edie finished, as she pulled her needle through the fabric.

Louise spoke again before Edie could continue with her favorite topic, crime in the neighborhoods.

"How about you, Edie? Would you like to come with me?"

"I'm sorry, but I can't. I'm going right over to the dentist from here." She raised her left hand from beneath the quilt and rubbed her fingers along her lower right jaw. "I'm having some pain from this tooth. I just hope I don't need a root canal."

"Oh dear." Anna was ever sympathetic.

"I'll go," Maggie offered. "I don't have any special plans for the afternoon." And she wouldn't mind having another look around the care center. Especially around the garden.

Clare couldn't hide her satisfied smile. "You are investigating again. I knew it. You wouldn't want to let Candy down."

Maggie frowned. "I just plan to keep Louise company. And visit Candy, of course."

But Clare wouldn't be convinced. Ever since Maggie had played an important role in discovering the killer of her son's friend, Clare had insisted on casting her in the role of Scottsdale's Jessica Fletcher.

"You should look around carefully while you're out there, Maggie. You too, Louise. See if you spot anything suspicious. I wish I could go with you." Clare released a deep sigh. "But Gerald wants me to go with him to pick out some new slacks. He really needs them, but he hates to shop. I have to go while he's in the mood."

"Harry was the same way," Maggie sympathized.

"If you're going home before you go to the care center, I have a suggestion," Edie said. "Rather than bringing back whatever Candy has sewn, just take an iron and a thick towel with you. There'll be a table in her room that you can use as an ironing board—just fold the towel over a few times and use it as padding. And if the iron is still warm when you leave, you can wrap it in the towel."

"Why, Edie." Maggie smiled at her. "What a wonderful idea."

Edie, embarrassed at the unaccustomed praise, shrugged. "I used to do that when we traveled. I have a small travel iron."

Edie rarely spoke about her married days. Maggie was even more surprised to hear her reference to travel. In all the years she'd known her, Edie had never taken a trip. And all they really knew about her past life was that she was widowed.

"I have a travel iron," Louise said. "That's an excellent idea. It will save a lot of time, and Candy can have her blocks back right away." She smiled at Victoria. "If she's as eager as you seem to think, she'll want to get right on with putting them together."

"I think she will." Victoria returned the smile. "She'll be so glad to see you both."

12

Maggie and Louise enjoyed lunch together before driving over to the care center. It worked out well that Maggie had not driven that morning, as she just went home with Louise and Vince when the Quilting Bee broke up. After lunch, Vince adjourned to his computer and the women spent a pleasant hour sorting through Louise's "stash," choosing fabrics and cutting them into squares for Candy's baby quilt.

Entering the care home's grounds, Maggie once again enjoyed the sight of the gardens adjacent to the parking lot. If there was only one gardener, he must be a very busy man.

Clare's story about the fake cook came back to her, but she quickly dismissed it. That was fiction, after all. The man who tended this garden was extremely good at what he did. Obviously a professional. But it didn't stop Maggie from peering intently into the garden while Louise parked the minivan. Fiction or not, she was interested in seeing this man Candy named as suspect. But the only people she could see, even those engaged in gardening activities, appeared to be patients.

"That breeze feels wonderful," Louise said, as they exited the car and started across the asphalt. "I knew it was going to be hot today, but the breeze makes it tolerable."

Maggie smiled. Unlike so many of the valley's residents,

Maggie was a native. The heat didn't bother her. In fact, she preferred it to the cold winter days of January.

"That breeze is nice. It's carrying over the scent of the roses." She glanced toward some rose bushes grouped near the building's entry and heavily laden with blossoms. The scent of roses brought back memories of the old ranch house where she'd lived for so many years, and the rose garden she'd cultivated there. It also suffused her with the peace she'd always found working among the thorny plants.

"Maybe I'll have time to go out to the ranch for a ride before dinner," Maggie said. "I went out yesterday, and it was wonderful. This weather is perfect for riding."

Thought of another afternoon ride through the desert brought a smile to Maggie's lips. Unlike the care center garden, there wouldn't be any colorful petunias or vincas to brighten the landscape. There wouldn't be any jacaranda trees, waving purple-blossomed limbs in the breeze, snowing petals on the ground to create a purple carpet. And there most certainly would not be the perfume of blooming rose bushes out on the desert trails where she would ride.

But the saguaros would be showing off their lovely white blossoms. There would be doves and cactus wrens and perhaps a hawk or two. There would be cholla cacti with their deceptively fuzzy look, ready to prick the unwary. The desert had its own beauty—different from the care center's lush garden, but equally lovely.

The mysterious gardener forgotten, Maggie took another appreciative sniff of the rose-scented air.

"It's a good day for a ride," Louise agreed. "And maybe Sara will invite you to join them for dinner."

"That would be nice. I ate with them last night, but I wouldn't mind doing it again." Maggie was always glad to join her son and his family for a meal. Sara was an excellent cook, and Maggie never tired of spending time with her grandsons. And not having to cook just for herself for a night was a nice treat as well. Not having to cook for two nights would be a double delight. Cooking for one was not something she enjoyed.

Maggie paused, looking back at the parking lot where a sleek black sports car stood in lonely grandeur toward the far end. It was far from any of the other cars parked there, and a long walk from the facility. There were numerous open spaces closer to the building, though the sporty car *was* parked in a shady spot.

"Look at that car at the back of the lot. Why would anyone want to park so far away?" Maggie asked.

"I've heard that some women park as far from the building as they can so that they have to walk the distance. It's how they keep their weight under control." Louise turned to look.

Maggie frowned. "Sounds like an interesting method. Could get a little hot around here though."

"That could be why it's way out there," Louise commented. "It's a nice shady spot. But it looks more like a man's car, doesn't it?"

"Candy drives a sports car," Maggie reminded her. "Do you think it's hers, that one of her kids is driving it?"

"Wasn't it badly damaged in the accident?" Louise asked. "Besides, Candy's was green."

"You're right," Maggie admitted. "I don't know how I could have forgotten about the accident. I'm sure she said the car was totaled."

Louise took another look at the car. "Maybe it's one of the workers."

"With a car like that?"

Louise grinned. "You're right. Nursing doesn't pay

enough for a car like that."

Maggie was still staring at the sleek black car.

"Doesn't that car look familiar?" Maggie frowned. It was possible the car just reminded her of Candy's since Candy was the only woman Maggie had ever known who drove an honest-to-goodness sports car.

"Probably because we just walked by one just like it," Louise told her. She pointed to a second car, this one dark blue, parked right in front of the entrance.

"Hmm. I didn't even see it."

"Sure you did." Louise grinned. "With your subconscious mind. That's why the other car seemed so familiar."

Maggie grinned as she stepped up to the door. "Think I should get myself a car like that?"

Louise's grin widened. "Go for it. But I want to be there when your sons see it for the first time."

Laughing, Maggie stepped inside, murmuring a soft thank you to Louise who held the door open for her. Then, the door still half open, they both stopped in confusion. Loud rock music blasted down the hall. Even here at the door, the volume was intense enough to tempt Maggie to put her hands over her ears.

Maggie and Louise looked at one another.

"Someone must be entertaining the patients," Louise suggested.

"A little loud, don't you think?"

"Maybe the patients are hard of hearing."

As though someone had heard Maggie's comment and acted on it, the volume of the music suddenly subsided to a mere roar.

"Well, that's a *little* better," Louise said. She moved in far enough to close the door.

Maggie nodded her agreement.

"Maybe we should check the day room first," Maggie suggested. "Candy might be there, if there's entertainment being provided."

"Good idea," Louise agreed.

They found the day room filled with both patients and staff. A group of teenagers clad in baggy jeans and white T-shirts were performing in a cleared area at the end of the room. Maggie smiled at the young men and women dancing in a style she recognized from her granddaughter's last recital as "hip hop." She had to chuckle at the varied looks of the patients, ranging from startled to amused to tolerant.

"I don't see her."

Louise's voice brought Maggie back to their errand. Distracted by the dancers, she hadn't checked the room for Candy. Now she did. She didn't see her either.

"I guess we'd better go to her room."

Maggie kept her voice lowered. Even though the music was loud, she didn't want to disturb the performers or their audience.

As they turned, Maggie saw Tara smile and wave. She returned the greeting, moving a few paces over so that she could say hello to her new friend.

The small gesture of politeness caused her to arrive at Candy's room a moment after Louise. Louise was already inside, standing beside the bed when Maggie entered. Candy lay in bed, her eyes closed. Louise held her wrist, her forehead wrinkled in concern.

"Is she asleep?" Maggie moved closer, hoping for an affirmative answer to her question.

But she was disappointed.

"I think you'd better call Tara right away."

Maggie stared. Louise had spoken in a firm, business-like voice. A no-nonsense, do-what-I-say voice.

Maggie had a dozen questions at least, but she moved immediately to obey Louise's order.

Walking quickly back to the common room, Maggie went directly to Tara's side and quietly asked her to come to Candy's room. Maggie wondered if Louise's urgency had passed on to her, for Tara left without a word and hurried down the hall.

Following her, Maggie still had time to note that a different group was now performing, six tap dancers all in black with glittering silver top hats.

"What is it?" Tara asked, though she didn't slow her pace.

"It's Candy," Maggie replied. "Louise asked me to get you right away."

There wasn't time to say more. They were already at Candy's door. Louise still stood beside the bed, but she was administering CPR. Tara rushed to the bed. Felt for a pulse. "Call 911," she tossed over her shoulder to Maggie.

13

Later, on the telephone with Victoria, Maggie was amazed at her clear memories of the afternoon. In Candy's room, with Tara and Louise busy at the bed, Maggie made the phone call, then remained standing beside the phone, almost flat against the wall. Numb with shock, she stood there, out of the way and forgotten. She'd admired Louise's quick action, her steady demeanor throughout. When it was time to leave, Maggie was grateful that she had not driven to the care center; she felt shaken by the experience of seeing a friend die. Louise, however, with her nursing background and years of emergency room experience, remained stalwart.

"She'd done a lot of stitching," Maggie told Victoria. She didn't know how she remembered this, but she could see Candy's new basket filled to overflowing. "The basket we gave her was on the bedside table, just filled with completed four-patch blocks."

"Then her last hours were probably happy ones," Victoria observed. "She spent them stitching those blocks for her future grandchild's quilt. She must have worked on them last night and this morning. You know how exciting it is to work on a new project."

"You're right. I hadn't thought of that." Maggie paused. "We should get those blocks from Andrea and make them into a baby quilt. Then Nathan's child can still have a quilt from his grandmother."

"Good idea." Victoria's voice softened. "And how are you? Would you like me to come over for a while?"

Maggie smiled. "No, but thanks. I'm okay. I'm making a cup of tea." Maggie knew that Victoria would smile at this. Tea was their mutual answer to anxiety and disaster.

"It's funny how it's all coming back now though. While I was there, watching Louise and Tara do CPR, then the paramedics taking over and wheeling her out . . . I just felt numb, I guess. I didn't think I was really seeing anything except that frantic activity."

"Are you sure you don't want to come over?"

Maggie could hear the concern in her friend's voice, and her heart swelled with this sign of their friendship.

"I'm all right. Really."

The shrill whistle of the tea kettle distracted her. Victoria heard it too. "Your water is ready."

"Yes." Maggie took the kettle from the stove and poured the boiling water into her teapot, where two tea bags already hung. She had decided on her best china pot and teacup. Chamomile tea in good china seemed so civilized; it was what she needed right now.

"You know what I've been seeing?"

"Oh, Maggie . . ."

"No, no, it's not what you're thinking." Maggie returned the kettle to the stove and put the cover on the teapot to let it steep. She sat, resting her elbow on the table.

"What I keep remembering is the scene outside Candy's window."

Maggie paused, but Victoria saw no need to fill the brief silence. Maggie felt sure she was turning her mind back to her own visits with Candy, picturing the prospect outside the large window.

"Inside, the room was full of people, frantic with activity. There was a lot of noise from the medical personnel. And they had a visiting dance group there, entertaining the patients, so loud music was coming from the day room down the hall. I plastered myself against the wall and tried to keep out of the way. From where I stood, I had a clear view out the window, into that lovely garden. Out there it was quiet and calm and peaceful. There was a hummingbird, flitting among the honeysuckle blossoms. And across the lawn, there was a bed of petunias. Red and white and purple. The plants were small and the soil between them was a deep black, like they had just been put in, and with lots of mulch."

She ended with a heavy sigh.

"A pretty, tranquil scene."

"Yes."

"Quite a contrast to what was happening there beside you. I'm not surprised you remember it. The mind does some strange things, but I'm sure it's easier on you to recall the flowers in the garden, than to remember the people inside who were trying so hard to save Candy's life."

There was a moment of silence as Maggie poured out her tea. She took a sip before returning to her conversation. Victoria was comfortable with the silence and waited it out.

"I don't understand it. She seemed to be in excellent health when we saw her yesterday."

"You don't think . . ."

Victoria didn't finish her sentence, but Maggie knew immediately what she was thinking. She'd thought it herself.

"Oh, no. That Angel of Death thing is just too outlandish."

Victoria's voice was thoughtful. "It is strange, though."

"Hmm." Maggie considered it for a moment. But, no. It was just too much to believe. "No, Victoria. I'm sure that whole Angel of Death thing was just an idea she and her friend Rhonda picked up from that TV show—something to make the time there more interesting. Some people like to scare themselves."

Maggie heard the words coming from her mouth, in her voice, but she could hear Michael saying them. Was she trying to talk herself into going along with his point of view?

But Victoria wasn't buying any of it.

"Not Candy," she replied. "She never went to scary movies or read Stephen King."

There wasn't much to say to that. Maggie knew it was true. It had been her argument against Michael. But she could play devil's advocate. "Maybe it was her friend Rhonda, and she just dragged Candy in with her."

"Maybe."

"And don't forget those other deaths she told us about, the ones they felt were suspicious," Maggie said. "Those all occurred at night."

Victoria had to concede that point. But Maggie knew that her friend still had doubts. How could she not, when Maggie herself had them?

14

When Maggie got off the phone with Victoria, she spent some thoughtful time sipping her tea. The warm liquid soothed her almost as much as talking to her old friend. But there was one troublesome aspect to the conversation. Sensible, conservative Victoria bringing up Candy's Angel of Death was worth a moment of contemplation.

Maggie tried to remember everything Candy had told them about the television program and her own suspicions. She still couldn't understand how they could translate the television example to their own situation. That person had been killing terminally ill patients to spare them more pain. To allow them to die with dignity. The patients at Palo Verde were not so ill. Most were merely incapacitated. As far as she knew, none of the patients there were completely bedridden.

Maggie took another sip of her tea and shook her head. In addition, as she'd mentioned to Victoria, the deaths at the center that Candy recounted had all occurred at night. That was the major difference she could see insofar as Candy's death was concerned. Candy had died in the afternoon.

Maggie thought of her brief conversation on the subject with Michael on Monday night. The arguments she seemed to be repeating as she'd talked to Victoria. Monday seemed so long ago. Michael had brushed off any suspicions she'd had, but what would he think now?

Deciding that this couldn't wait, Maggie refilled her teapot with hot water, topped up her pretty china cup, and reached for the phone. Surprisingly, Michael picked up himself.

"Michael. I thought I'd have to leave a message."

"Hi, Ma. I'm off today. I've been getting stuff done around the house."

"Good for you."

Maggie paused. How to start? She took a sip of her tea, and promptly put the cup down. The tea in her newly refilled cup was very hot.

With a quiet sigh she hoped Michael couldn't hear, Maggie soothed her scorched tongue with an inhaled breath and decided it was probably best to plunge right into her story.

"Michael, Candy Breckner died this afternoon."

"Oh, Ma. I'm sorry. I know she was a friend of yours."

Maggie accepted his condolences, but then frowned. How to approach the other. Probably better get right to the point. Michael would be sure to see through any attempt to tease a comment from him.

"Remember how I told you that she was afraid to stay there in the care center?"

She could hear her son's sigh. It made her smile. But it didn't diminish her concern.

"Not that Angel of Death thing?"

Maggie heard the condescension in his voice. Really, adult children could be very trying.

"That was *my* first reaction too. But since then I've been thinking. Michael, she was so frightened. And Victoria and I were just out to see her on Wednesday. She looked very well, and was excited by a quilting project we brought for her to work on."

"Strokes and heart attacks can happen to anyone, Ma. At anytime. Anything can bring it on, including excitement. Remember that high school football player in Mesa last year? Died right on the field during practice. Had a heart attack. No warning. And he was a supposedly healthy seventeen year old."

"Yes, I do remember." She also heard what he wasn't saying. That Candy was an elderly woman. An old lady. Much more likely to die from a heart attack or a stroke. Not unexpected at all.

"And she'd just been in an accident. Sometimes people die after accidents—hours later, or days later. They get blood clots, but the clots take a while to work their way into the heart or lungs."

Maggie sighed. "Okay, maybe I'm just getting carried away because she was so worried. Still, she looked so good yesterday. Even this afternoon, we thought she was just asleep . . ."

"You mean you found the body?"

Michael's voice rose enough that Maggie's hand holding the receiver automatically pulled away from her ear.

"Didn't I mention that?"

Maggie returned the receiver to her ear as she finished her comment. From the indistinct muttering coming from the other end of the phone line, Maggie determined that she had not mentioned it.

"Louise and I went over this afternoon to take her more supplies. We're—we were," she corrected herself, "helping Candy with a quilt project. Something to keep her busy while she was in the care center. We thought it would distract her."

"That was a good thought. But I take it she still believed this Angel of Death was at work there."

"I'm afraid so." Maggie sighed; she seemed to be doing a lot of it this afternoon. "We overheard her talking to Andrea yesterday, before we went into the room. She was crying, pleading with her to take her home before 'he' killed her."

"And today?" Michael asked.

"Louise and I went over there this afternoon with some fabric. Yesterday Victoria and I took Candy a basket filled with fabric squares, and thread, and everything she needed to start a small quilt. She wanted more bright colors, and we said we'd bring more, and take the blocks she'd finished to iron." Maggie pushed at the handle of her teacup, spinning it on its saucer. "There was a noisy dance demonstration going on in the day room, so we checked there first. The room was filled, but she wasn't in there. So we went to her room, and she was lying in bed. Louise was the first one in . . ."

"Well, thank goodness for that."

Maggie stopped playing with the teacup, dropping her hand onto her lap.

"It wasn't bad, Michael. As I said, I thought she was sleeping. If Louise hadn't sent me right out to get Tara, and sounded so, well, serious about it . . ."

Maggie could hear Michael's large sigh. "And who is Tara?"

"She's the head nurse. She went to school with Bobby only she was Tara McClintock then, not Tara Dillion. Anyway, Tara came right away and had me call 911. The paramedics took Candy away."

Maggie's voice faded as she reached the end of her tale. She felt tired now. Perhaps the day was catching up with her.

"Well." Michael paused.

Maggie could almost see his face as he considered all she'd said. If he had been in the room with her, he'd be checking her out, looking for signs that she was upset, or fatigued.

"You've had quite a day, Ma. Maybe you should make yourself a cup of tea, relax."

Maggie had to smile. "I'm doing that now." She raised her cup to her lips. This time the liquid was the perfect temperature—hot, but not scorching. The soothing tea slid down her throat, warming her insides. Maggie's smile widened. She did feel better.

"About that Angel of Death . . ."

Maggie's smile vanished; the teacup returned to its saucer with a clatter. Surprised that Michael had returned to the subject, Maggie straightened her spine. As if sitting upright could improve her hearing ability!

"I still don't think there's anything in it. She and her friends were probably just trying to make their time there more interesting. I'm sure the days seem long and pass slowly to someone in a convalescent home." Michael's voice softened. "In a day or two, you'll learn that Mrs. Breckner died of natural causes. Then you can put this whole Angel of Death thing to rest."

Maggie could hear the love coming through the phone line as he tried to comfort her. It made her feel better than she had all day. She was certainly blessed in her sons.

They spoke for a few minutes longer, mainly about the rest of the family. But thoughts of an Angel of Death continued to trouble Maggie's mind.

When Michael asked if he should call Bobby and tell him about Candy, Maggie said she would do it.

As she dialed his number, Maggie wondered if Bobby

and Andrea had kept in touch. It was one of the first things she asked, after she told him her reason for calling.

"It's the usual story, Ma," Bobby told her. "When we graduated, our group all said we'd keep in touch. And we did get together every summer for a while. But then our lives started going in different directions. We had graduate school or internships or jobs. People started getting married. And pretty soon we were just sending cards at Christmas time."

Maggie nodded, even though she realized Bobby was unable to see her gesture. Many of her friendships had undergone the same process.

"So you haven't seen her lately." It was more a statement than a question.

"We run into each other now and then. When we do, we talk. But we haven't had a good long visit since the last reunion."

"You're both young," Maggie said. "Your lives are so full of work and family and recreation, I'm not surprised."

"I'm sorry to hear about her mom, though. I don't think her marriage is in the best shape, so it's going to be hard for her."

Maggie wasn't sure what to say. "Do you know Alan?"

"Just a nodding acquaintance. But last time I saw Andrea she was really upset. I ran into her at the drugstore, and had to say something. She looked like she'd been crying. She tried to say it was allergies, but then she finally admitted she'd had a fight with Alan."

"That's too bad. She'll need his support now."

"Yeah. Let's hope they've patched things up." His voice didn't sound too hopeful.

"Let me know when the funeral is, Ma. I guess it will be at St. Rose." Bobby's voice rose at the end of the sentence, turning the supposition into a question.

"I'm sure it will be. But since she just passed away this afternoon, I can't say for sure. Or when it will be. I'll let you know as soon as I hear."

They spoke for a few more minutes, their conversation ending before Maggie realized that she hadn't told Bobby about meeting Tara. She'd have to remember to tell him on Sunday, when the family got together for brunch.

Maggie continued to sit for a while after disconnecting. She wondered if she should have said something to him about Candy's fears and premonitions. But in her head, she heard once again Michael's condescending tones when he talked about an old woman's delusions. She wondered if Michael realized that she was even older than Candy. Only a year, but still, older. It was enough to make her reconsider dwelling on the Angel of Death theory. She wouldn't want to give her sons reason to think she was getting paranoid. Or worse yet, delusional.

15

"You actually found her body?"

Maggie had not gotten out to the ranch to have a ride on Chestnut the day before. She and Louise had stayed at the care home after the paramedics left with Candy. Tara provided cups of her excellent coffee, and they used the time to wind down and to reminisce about Candy.

At least, Maggie and Tara had reminisced. Maggie suddenly realized that Louise had been extremely quiet at their little session. Pale too. Of course, nurse or not, she had just had a difficult experience, seeing a friend near death and trying to save her. Tara had praised Louise for her quick action in starting CPR. Louise had accepted this graciously, but Maggie wondered if she felt some guilt about not being able to save her.

Shaking off memories of those unsettling hours, Maggie experienced a sudden feeling of bone-wearying tiredness. Once Louise returned her to her home yesterday, she had called various members of the Quilting Bee to tell them what had happened. Louise called others. With that and calls to family members, Maggie felt as if she'd spent the whole evening on the phone.

Now that they were all gathered at the quilting frame in the Bee room, the Bee members wanted to hear all the details from Maggie and Louise. Hearing it on the phone was one thing; hearing it in person somehow made it more real. Anna's comment had come with a little shudder. Maggie knew that Anna would *not* have enjoyed a similar experience.

"There was a dance presentation going on when we arrived," Maggie began. "What a racket! I'm surprised we didn't hear it in the parking lot."

"I think they were just starting when we opened the door," Louise injected.

Before Edie could begin expounding on the dangers of loud rock music, and the future deafness of today's youth, Maggie went on.

"We went into the day room thinking Candy would be in there with the others, watching the presentation. When we didn't see her, we went to her room."

All eyes turned to Louise, who sighed as she picked up her newly threaded needle and began to sew. She kept her eyes on the quilt top.

"I got to her room first, and I just sensed there was something wrong."

Maggie felt obligated to explain her delay. "I saw Tara as we were leaving the day room, and stopped to say hello."

Clare, holding a needle but barely stitching at all, turned back to Louise. But Maggie wasn't finished.

"I thought Candy was sleeping. If not for Louise and her professional knowledge, I'm sure I would have just sat down and waited for her to wake up." She shook her head. "It would have been a long wait."

"It was mostly intuition," Louise said softly.

"She didn't seem ill when we saw her on Wednesday," Victoria said. "Has anyone heard about the cause of death?"

Maggie turned an admiring glance toward Victoria. What a diplomatic turn of phrase!

"Was it a stroke?" Clare asked. "Candy did have high blood pressure."

Maggie expressed her surprise that Clare would have this information when the rest of them did not. But Clare merely shrugged.

"She talked about her medication with me. She knew I took pills for high blood pressure too."

"Tara seemed to think it was a stroke," Louise said.

Maggie glanced up. Something in Louise's tone caused her to pause in her stitching. "You don't think it was a stroke?"

Louise frowned. "It's certainly possible. But I don't know." Louise shook her head as though trying to clear it of some odd thought. Or perhaps to knock one loose. "I guess it's just a feeling I have that something wasn't quite right."

"Was it a smell of bitter almonds?" Clare asked eagerly.

Although the question was asked in all seriousness, the others laughed. Maggie laughed so hard she felt a stitch in her side. Clare looked offended at first, but then the others' mirth caught her too and she chuckled.

"I guess that was a silly question," Clare admitted.

"Oh, Clare. Thank you." Maggie reached over and placed her hand over Clare's arm. "It was a stressful afternoon and evening, and I sure did need that laughter."

Louise nodded. "We all needed it." She directed a smile toward Clare. "And, no, it wasn't bitter almonds. I'm sure I wouldn't know what bitter almonds smelled like anyhow."

Clare shrugged, admitting with some disappointment that she probably wouldn't recognize it either. "They always say that in books, though."

"Yes, they do," Victoria agreed. "But this isn't a book, Clare. Why would anyone want to kill Candy? With cyanide of all things. She was just an ordinary woman who was recovering from an accident. She wouldn't hurt anyone."

"It's all guns nowadays," Edie said. A decisive nod and a pull of her thread punctuated her statement. "Gangs and guns."

"What about the Angel of Death?"

Silence greeted Anna's quietly spoken question. They had all been thinking of the Angel of Death, of course. But apparently the others were as hesitant as Maggie to bring it up.

"Do you think there really was an Angel of Death?" Maggie asked.

"I saw that show she was talking about," Victoria said. "It was about a man in a hospital in California, a nurse. He was killing the really sick patients. With potassium chloride, I think it was. Putting it in their IVs, so that they died quietly in their sleep. He thought he was being kind, putting them out of their pain, allowing them to die with some dignity. I don't know how Candy jumped from that to the conclusion that someone at her facility was killing people. None of them were terribly ill. There were no IVs to inject."

"Do you think being involved in that accident affected her mind?" Anna asked.

The women stitched quietly while they considered this. Through the open door, they heard the water spraying into the fountain, the birds singing in the olive tree.

Victoria's gentle voice was the first to break the peace of the moment.

"Some people find it easy to imagine that anything they hear about applies to them." Victoria kept her eyes down, examining her last stitches. Satisfied with what she saw, she straightened and continued, with both her stitching and her conversation. "It's very common with people who read about the symptoms of an illness."

Maggie looked to Louise, who nodded. They'd discussed

this earlier in the week.

"So you think she was just imagining it?" Anna asked.

No one needed to be told that Anna was referring to Candy and her so-called Angel of Death.

"Don't you?" Maggie's voice was even. She didn't want to influence the others with her own opinion. "Can you really believe that someone in that lovely facility was killing the patients?"

Maggie couldn't help but see those lovely halls, the beautiful garden, the contented looks on the faces of the patients she saw in the halls. Though she had to admit that Candy hadn't been one of the satisfied patients.

No one said anything. Even Edie seemed hesitant to agree with Candy.

"You should investigate, Maggie." Clare's voice was firm but her eyes sparkled. "Maybe the Angel of Death killed poor Candy."

Maggie snipped off a thread and examined the circular feather design she'd just completed in one of the alternate nine-patch blocks. She brushed a stray thread from the fabric and stood, sliding her chair to the right so that she could begin work on another block.

"I'm not convinced there's anything there to investigate," Maggie said.

"You could start with the gardener," Clare added.

Maggie settled herself back in her chair. "I finally saw him."

Several exclamations greeted this revelation.

"Where?"

"When?"

"Why didn't you tell us?"

Maggie waited for the barrage of questions to stop, calmly inserting her needle into the quilt sandwich and beginning to stitch in the new block.

"I didn't speak to him. I saw him from the window in Candy's room yesterday. When everyone was around the bed, trying to help Candy and things were so frantic. I was standing to the side, trying to stay out of the way. I think everyone forgot I was even there. And I looked out the window. There was a lovely peaceful view from her window—into that beautiful garden."

"I thought the same thing when we were there," Victoria acknowledged.

"Did you notice the honeysuckle?" Anna asked. "They were blooming so nicely, just outside the window. Such a shame the window didn't open. The scent would have been lovely."

"Probably just give her a headache," Edie commented. "Or make her sneeze."

"Oh, I don't think Candy had allergies," Anna responded. "She loved flowers of all kinds."

Maggie hid a smile.

Clare pulled her thread, then held the needle above the quilt top for a moment while she brought the conversation back to her area of interest. "Well, we know something already. The gardener, the person Candy suspected might kill her, was right outside her room when it happened." Clare turned to Anna. "Are you sure the windows didn't open?"

"Oh, yes, I'm sure. They didn't. I commented on the lovely flowers to Candy; told her she should open the window so that she could enjoy the fragrance. And she told me they didn't open at all. Said they were probably afraid they would escape out the window."

"I'm sure she was making a joke," Maggie said.

"Not altogether," Louise said. "A facility of that type would have to be very careful about doors and windows.

110

They probably have Alzheimer's patients who could wander off and become lost. In fact weren't there patients working out in the garden when we were there? I've heard that's one of the latest things in treating Alzheimer's patients—letting them garden. They enjoy it."

Maggie made a mental note to ask Tara about that next time she saw her. Then promptly scolded herself. Why would she be seeing Tara again if she weren't getting involved?

Meanwhile Louise was still speaking.

"And sometimes medications can make people disoriented."

"Maybe Candy's medications were making her delusional," Clare suggested. "If there isn't an Angel of Death."

"Do you know if she was taking anything?" Maggie asked.

Clare shook her head.

"She may have had some pain medication," Louise said. "But since it had been a while since her accident, I'm not sure she would have still been getting it. They like to be careful with the pain meds."

"Wouldn't the nurse—your friend, Maggie—have checked on that?" Edie asked. "You told us that Candy mentioned the Angel of Death to her too."

"She seemed to think it was just Candy's imagination working overtime." Maggie frowned. "And she seemed more interested in letting me know they would never have any problems like that at her facility."

A movement at the door caught Maggie's eye as she finished speaking. She jumped to her feet, cutting Edie off as she began to speak of care homes in general.

"Andrea!" Maggie called, hurrying toward the door.

16

"I'm so sorry about your mother." Maggie gestured at the other Bee members, now all standing around the quilt frame or approaching Andrea and Maggie at the door. "We all are."

Andrea acknowledged their sympathy, but seemed hesitant about entering the room. "Don't let me disturb you."

"Don't be silly," Maggie said. "You must know you're welcome anytime."

"Of course," Louise echoed. "We're sewing, but we're also visiting. In fact, we were just talking about your mother."

Maggie nodded. "We had all been out to see her this week you know."

Andrea seemed to stiffen. The movement was so slight, Maggie wasn't even sure she saw it. The younger woman's body just seemed to pull back, then relax again.

Andrea took a step into the room and looked from Maggie to Louise. She looked uncomfortable, and cleared her throat before speaking.

"I know you were the ones who, ah, found her." She changed the wide strap of her purse from one shoulder to the other. "Tara Dillion told me that you did all that you could."

As Maggie and Louise said the required things, Andrea

finally stepped fully inside the room. Her eyes moved over the quilt frame, the chairs, the closet filled with supplies.

"Mom loved coming here and working with all of you."

Close to the frame now, Andrea let her fingers trail along one of the quilted feather circles that filled the plain white block of the quilt. Her voice grew soft as she took in the delicate stitching and the blue and white pieced blocks. "She would have loved working on this quilt. Blue was always a favorite of hers."

Andrea turned quickly. Maggie wondered if she was embarrassed by her brief sentimental moment. By the time she reached the door and turned back to face them, she was once again her brisk, efficient self. The consummate businesswoman.

"I called Father Bob yesterday about the funeral arrangements. I was hoping for tomorrow."

"So soon!" Anna's comment was little more than a murmur, but Andrea heard her.

"There's no point in waiting." Her voice was crisp. "And I have so much to do—it's an especially busy time of year for me at work. We end our fiscal year on the thirty-first."

Maggie still stood near the door, but she wished she were back at the frame with the others. She'd like to pick up her needle and continue her stitching, try to forget she'd heard that. Andrea made it sound like she couldn't make time in her life to mourn her mother's death.

"However," Andrea continued, "it will have to wait until Monday. Because her death was unexpected, there has to be an autopsy." She shuddered. "I hate to even think of it."

Maggie noticed the quiver of Andrea's shoulders and felt better. At least she seemed to have a daughter's normal reaction to the idea of an autopsy on her mother's body.

Anna was having a similar response. "An autopsy! How awful."

"But why?" Clare asked. "Do they suspect something?"

Andrea frowned. "What would they suspect?" Then she seemed to realize what Clare meant. "Oh, no, I'm sure there was nothing suspicious about her death. I was told that the police look into all deaths that happen unexpectedly."

"So it wasn't because of her Angel of Death suspicions," Clare said.

Andrea looked at the women and frowned. "I can't believe she told all of you about that." She shook her head. "I hope you didn't believe any of it. She saw that program on television and it just made her crazy. That's all I can imagine anyway, the way she reacted to it."

"I don't think anyone did take her seriously," Maggie replied. She shot a quelling glance toward Clare, willing her not to contradict her. "But I just wondered. Was it a general fear she had, or had she centered on one individual?" Maggie didn't mention that Candy had named someone to Victoria.

Andrea sighed. "She seemed to think it was one of the nursing assistants. A young man named Joseph."

Maggie exchanged surprised looks with the other Bee members, but Andrea didn't appear to notice. She continued to speak.

"I met him several times and he seemed like a nice person. Polite, joked a little. Had a nice way about him with the patients, I thought. Kind of flirted with the older ladies, you know?"

Maggie suppressed the flash of irritation she felt at this last. He sounded patronizing to her. Then she realized he was the young man she'd seen that day in the staff lounge, the young man who had been asleep on the sofa when she and Tara came into the room. The one with the charming smile. The same one Tara had indicated might be fired if good help was easier to find.

"The other patients seem to like Joseph a lot. I don't know why Mother didn't. That's why she spent so much time in her room."

Andrea noted Maggie's quizzical look and answered the unspoken question.

"Joseph was the one they would send in to take her into the common room, or out to the garden to sit. Once she got this strange idea about him, she wouldn't let him help her."

"I see." What Andrea said matched what Tara had already told her about Candy and Joseph. It certainly explained Candy's extreme reaction to him. But what could have gotten into Candy to accuse two entirely different men?

"To let you know how irrational mother was getting, she told Nathan and Stephanie that she suspected Tara. She never mentioned that to me, or even that she had any other suspects besides Joseph." Andrea looked at Maggie, the intensity of her gaze causing Maggie to glance back at the others.

Maggie met Victoria's eyes. And sighed. Victoria shrugged. Candy had named three different people.

As the puzzled Bee members exchanged surprised but silent looks, Andrea checked her watch. Maggie suspected she was anxious to leave. But Andrea surprised Maggie by remaining at the door, her hand clutching the strap of her purse. Then she turned so that she was fully facing the women at the quilt frame.

"While I'm here . . . I wonder if I could impose on you all."

She was speaking to all of the Bee women, but her gaze finally rested on Maggie who remained beside her.

"I guess it depends on what it is you want," Maggie replied lightly. She had no idea what Andrea might be leading up to. And she wasn't feeling especially charitable toward her at the moment. Maggie couldn't decide if Andrea's haste over the funeral arrangements indicated pain, and a desire to move beyond it, or if it was merely an imposition into her busy lifestyle.

"I've been over to mother's since . . ."

Andrea paused for a brief moment before continuing and Maggie decided it might be pain after all.

". . . Ah, I was there this morning. And there's a lot to be done before the house can be sold."

Surprise verging on shock was the prevalent feeling around the quilting frame. Candy had not been gone even twenty-four hours and already she was talking about selling her house.

"You're not going to keep the house then," Edie said.

Maggie wondered if Andrea noticed the disapproving tone. It was none of Edie's business, after all. But Andrea didn't seem offended.

"No. The house actually belonged to my stepfather, mother's second husband. It will go to Nathan and Stephanie. But meanwhile, I have to remove her things. Over half the contents of the house are mother's."

"Will you get a service to go through and host a sale?" Victoria asked.

Andrea seemed startled by the suggestion. "Oh, no. I wouldn't want to do that. I'd have to be there to supervise. . . . I just don't have the time." She toyed nervously with the strap of her shoulder bag, moving it once again from one shoulder to the other.

Maggie frowned. Again, the time factor.

"The favor I wanted to ask was whether some of you ladies might be willing to go through her sewing room for me. I'm afraid I don't sew and I don't know what half the things in there are even for. And there's a lot of fabric . . ." She took a deep breath and looked around the room once again. Her glance rested for a moment on their supply closet. "If you'd be willing to go through her sewing things for me you could take whatever supplies you need for the Senior Guild."

There were exclamations of appreciation and thanks from the women for her generosity.

"I'd need a receipt of course," Andrea added. "For the taxes."

Maggie saw Edie raise an eyebrow, but she failed to comment. Too bad, Maggie thought. She could have made a few pithy remarks herself, but she might regret them later. Luckily, Victoria stepped in.

"That's very kind of you, donating all her supplies." Victoria put her needle into the top and stepped around the frame toward Andrea. "We'd be glad to do it."

The others nodded their agreement but remained sitting.

"When did you want us to come?" Maggie asked.

"Tomorrow would be fine," Andrea said. Then, apparently noting the startled look generated by her reply, she amended it. "Or anytime next week. Nathan is anxious to get the place cleaned up and on the market."

"Really?" Clare shot Maggie a look Maggie knew she meant as significant.

Andrea nodded. "He says the real estate market is hot right now and that homes in that area are really moving." She sighed. "His rush to sell is making it hard for me as I'm very busy at work right now. We're nearing the end of our fiscal year and there's a lot of paperwork and such. And of course there are all the extra things I have to do now because of mother's death."

Maggie wasn't sure she liked Andrea's attitude, but she wouldn't mind seeing Candy's sewing room.

"I might be able to come over tomorrow," Maggie said. "The Senior Guild doesn't meet on Saturdays, and I have some free time in the morning."

Victoria also agreed to go over, and soon all of the others jumped in. Everyone was anxious to see the supplies that would be coming to the Quilting Bee. New materials could spark the creative spirit.

Andrea looked relieved. "I didn't think to bring the key with me, but I'll be there at nine, to let you in. I can't thank you enough." She offered a swift smile, then glanced at her watch. Exclaiming over a meeting she was already late for, Andrea fled the room.

The Bee women looked after her with expressions ranging from bemusement to condemnation.

Edie's face held the fiercest aspect. "Well! As if her mother had chosen this time to die, just to vex her!"

Even Anna frowned. "I know she's a busy career woman, but you would think she could take a little time off after her mother's death." She shook her head, her eyes mournful. "Everyone is so busy nowadays. Such a shame."

"Candy was very proud of Andrea," Clare ventured.

"Though she did seem a tad irritated that she hadn't brought the needlework she'd requested to her at the care home." Maggie seated herself at the frame and picked up her needle, but looked around before she inserted it into the fabric. "Remember when she showed us that needlepoint piece she was working on?"

Clare remembered. "That's right. She said she'd asked

for her latest quilting project, but Andrea claimed that needlepoint kit was all she could find." She frowned. "She did seem a little irked about it."

"She just didn't want to be bothered," Edie declared. "Even someone who doesn't sew should know the difference between a quilt project and a needlepoint canvas. She's been around her mother and her sewing projects for all these years!"

Maggie had to agree. She noticed her friends' heads nodding as well.

"Do you think Andrea just didn't care that an Angel of Death might want to kill her mother?" Clare's voice was hushed with the incredulity of it.

"She just didn't want to take the time or the effort to really care for her," Edie said.

"We can't know that," Victoria countered. "Besides, none of us believed that story of hers; I'm sure Andrea didn't either."

"She really couldn't have cared for her at home with both her legs broken," Louise reminded them. "It's just unfortunate that Candy came up with this strange idea. And that she died so suddenly."

Maggie plied her needle with intent concentration. She didn't want to consider the possibilities. If there was an Angel of Death. If Candy had not died of natural causes.

Maggie remembered the red sky and the swooping owl then deliberately forced her attention back to her stitching. She always claimed not to believe in such superstitions. But, still . . .

Maggie didn't want her mind to go there.

17

Unfortunately, Maggie was forced to think of the possibilities later that afternoon. Detective Daryl Warner, whom she had met earlier in the year, appeared at her door. Maggie also knew that he was a homicide detective.

"Why, Detective Warner, won't you come in?" Maggie was the perfect hostess as she ushered him into her home, even though her mind raced with possible reasons for this visit. "Could I offer you a drink? I have soft drinks and iced tea, or I could make some coffee." In mystery books and on TV shows, the police were always drinking coffee. "It won't take long," she assured him.

"Thank you, but no. This is strictly a business call."

"Business?"

Maggie's body stiffened and a look of horror passed across her eyes. Michael! But didn't they send *two* officers to inform families of another officer's death?

Seeing her reaction and realizing what she must be thinking, Detective Warner took her arm and quickly reassured her.

"This has nothing to do with your son, Mrs. Browne. I just want to ask you some questions about events at the Palo Verde Care Center. I believe you were there yesterday afternoon."

As he spoke, Detective Warner led Maggie to the sofa,

then seated himself on an adjacent chair. Maggie was grateful for his gallant act; relief at learning this visit was not about Michael's death or injury had turned her knees weak. Maggie sank thankfully into the comfort of the familiar cushions, then turned to the detective.

"I was at the care center yesterday. A friend and I went to visit Candy Breckner. However, she passed away just before we arrived." Maggie shifted slightly, to give herself a better view of her guest. "Her daughter said something about the police looking into unexpected deaths."

Maggie watched Detective Warner carefully, but he gave nothing away.

"Police reports are filed on all unexpected deaths," he agreed. "Could you please tell me about your visit there? From the time you arrived?"

Maggie looked at him. She wanted to ask what he'd learned but she knew from previous acquaintance that Detective Warner was not only close-mouthed, but he had an excellent poker face. She stifled a sigh and began to describe her visit the previous afternoon. As she spoke, a sick feeling began to form in the pit of her stomach. Intuition told her something was dreadfully wrong.

Detective Warner jotted down a few notes as Maggie spoke. As she finished, he looked up briefly. "And how long was Mrs. Lombard alone in the room with Mrs. Breckner?"

Maggie's stomach lurched. Did he think she was a fool? She realized the implication of his question. Maggie wanted to shout that Louise was a wonderful, kind woman who would never harm another human being. But she allowed the space of two slow breaths to calm down. When she spoke, she felt in control. Calm. Inquiring.

"Is there something here I don't know? I was under the impression that Candy died of natural causes."

Detective Warner merely repeated what he'd said earlier. "It's normal procedure to inquire about any unexpected deaths." He looked calmly into her eyes. "Now, about Mrs. Lombard . . ."

Maggie glared at him. It sounded to her like he suspected Louise had done something to Candy. And he knew it.

Calm, Maggie reminded herself. Be calm.

"Louise was alone in the room for a minute, two at the most. As I told you, we drove over together and walked into the building together. There was loud music coming from the day room, so we headed there first. We thought all the patients would be in there; it was obvious they were having some kind of entertainment. But we didn't see Candy. We started out together, to go to her room, but then I stopped for a moment to say hello to Tara Dillion."

"The head nurse."

Maggie nodded.

"Did Ms. Dillion go down to Mrs. Breckner's room with you?"

"No. I told you I called her later. Louise asked me to get her when I went into Candy's room. Louise is a nurse. She saw that there was a problem and started CPR."

"Did you go up to Mrs. Breckner yourself? To see that she wasn't breathing?"

Maggie was startled by the question. The implication quickly hit her. "No, I took her word for it that there was a problem, and went immediately to get Tara. Time was essential. She was already starting CPR. I wasn't gone for more than a minute. Two at the most. I moved quickly, and Tara did too."

Detective Warner nodded and closed his notebook.

Maggie watched him. She had a bad feeling about this. She decided to tell him about Candy.

"Has anyone told you about Candy and her fears? About the Angel of Death she claimed was prowling the care center?"

Detective Warner reopened his notebook. "An Angel of Death? Someone killing patients you mean?"

Maggie nodded. She then recounted all the details she had about Candy and her theory. She even mentioned how Candy told Victoria about her suspicions regarding the gardener. She debated leaving it there, but then decided to tell him about Joseph and Tara as well. He'd better know it all. And if Candy's death had been unnatural, she'd be giving him three more suspects.

If Maggie thought Detective Warner was going to credit her for giving him great insight into his case, she was disappointed. He merely thanked her for her cooperation, pocketed his notebook, and left.

Maggie flew to the phone. Louise's answering machine picked up. Maggie left a message asking Louise to call her right away, then dialed Victoria's. Victoria's machine picked up.

Maggie left a brief "call me" message and pressed the disconnect button in frustration. Where was everyone?

Her question wasn't answered until Victoria returned her call some twenty minutes later.

"Victoria! Where were you?"

"Maggie." Victoria's voice was rife with concern. "What's wrong?"

Maggie took a deep breath. The pressure in her abdomen increased. Louise! A murder suspect! She might be jumping to conclusions—she hoped she was—but her intuition told her not.

"A homicide detective was just here, Victoria. Remember Detective Warner?"

"Yes." Victoria's voice remained calm. "He was here too. He just left. That's why I didn't answer the phone when you called earlier."

"Did he ask you about Louise?"

"Louise? No. At least not specifically. He asked me general questions about our visits to Candy before she died. Though now that I think about it, he did seem quite interested in that little dustup between Candy and Louise on Monday."

"I'm worried, Victoria." Quickly, Maggie told Victoria about the questions she had been asked. Victoria, too, instantly saw the implication.

"Oh, dear. But you didn't see any blood or anything. And you said the paramedics seemed to think it was natural causes."

"Yes," Maggie agreed. "But Andrea mentioned an autopsy. And with the questions Detective Warner was asking, it sounds like it might be murder. He didn't really say anything, but why else would he be emphasizing who was alone with her, and for how long? And he asked if I saw that she wasn't breathing before I called for help."

Victoria's voice was soft and calm.

"Andrea said they have to investigate when someone dies so suddenly. It was probably all routine. It's just that we heard Candy whining about death and killing, so we're more suspicious." She paused. "Though Detective Warner did ask about the Angel of Death."

"I told him about that."

"I did too. There isn't any reason not to. Candy seemed to be telling everyone."

"You're right. I just have this awful feeling . . ."

"You're not letting those so-called omens of doom influence you?"

Maggie recalled the gloomy red sky and the swooping owl. "I didn't think so. But at this stage I'm not sure of anything."

"It's probably just Candy's attitude that's influencing you. Why she acted like she was involved in an espionage case the way she whispered and kept checking the door." Victoria laughed. "Try to remember that we thought the whole thing was ridiculous at the time."

Maggie knew Victoria was right.

"Okay, I'll accept that theory for the moment. But," Maggie hesitated. "Could she have been murdered? And still look peaceful and asleep when we arrived?"

"We'll have to ask Louise. Perhaps something like pills, or poison."

"I think with poison the victim tends to vomit." Maggie was trying to recall all she had seen that afternoon. She was certain there was nothing about Candy's room or bed that was at all unusual. Without Louise, Maggie would have assumed she was asleep.

"It probably depends on the type of poison," Victoria observed.

Maggie pushed aside emotion and concentrated. "I'm sure there was nothing unusual about the bed." Once again she pictured the pretty room. "She might have been suffocated I suppose."

Victoria inhaled sharply. "Is that how victims in Angel of Death cases are killed?"

Could it be? Was Candy right after all?

"I don't know," Maggie finally admitted. "I think there are different methods. Wasn't there something about medicine in the IVs? In that program you saw?"

There was a brief moment of silence over the phone line as they thought about Candy's fears and her sudden death.

"Well, we did tell Detective Warner about Candy's fears and theories."

Maggie knew Victoria was trying to soothe her by reminding her that they had already done something constructive.

"I'm still worried about Louise." Maggie sighed. "What on earth can we do?"

Victoria's answer came as a surprise. But Maggie felt it validated her fears.

Victoria's voice was firm. "If they keep heading in this direction, we'll just have to find out who killed Candy ourselves."

18

Maggie wasn't able to contact Louise that afternoon. Restless, she started a batch of "Aggression Cookies," working on the dough as her mind wrestled with impossible-to-answer questions. "Aggression Cookies" were what she had turned to when her young children needed an outlet for inner frustrations. Mixing the dough was done entirely by hand, and little hands and fists could squeeze and pound at the ingredients in a most satisfactory manner. Maggie wasn't attacking the dough with her fists, but the physical action of mixing the ingredients, pressing the butter and dry ingredients together with her hands, was better than pacing the floor in frustration.

Maggie released a fistful of dough and grabbed for another. Was it possible Louise had been arrested? Could there be any real evidence that pointed to her?

Squeezing the dough through her fingers, Maggie was sure that if there was, it had to be flimsy at the very least. Not only had she known Louise for many years, she had been there when they found Candy. She *knew* there was no reason to suspect Louise.

Maggie had time to think things over as she formed the dough into balls and placed them on the cookie sheets. The careful but repetitive action left her mind free to think over the situation with Candy and Louise. She *knew* Louise was not a murderer. So if Candy had indeed been murdered, who could have done it? Maggie was aware that real homicides were usually much simpler than the complicated plots developed for movies and books. Real murders were usually committed by people known to the victim. And love/jealousy, money and revenge were the usual reasons. Scratch the first in Candy's case. And no matter how hard she thought, Maggie could not imagine any way that revenge could play into it. That left money. Maggie suspected that money played a large part in the majority of murder cases.

But money didn't seem to fit into the equation either. None of the Angel of Death suspects would profit from Candy's death. Only family normally did that. Unless Candy had written some sort of bequest into her will. But she really hadn't been there long enough for that. And with her unhappiness over the care center, and her accusations against the staff, it didn't seem likely that she would do such a thing anyway.

Maggie placed the last ball of dough onto the cookie sheet, flattened it, then washed her hands. She would have lots of cookies for the family brunch on Sunday, but she had no more insight into Candy's death now than she had had an hour ago.

With the last of the cookies in the oven, Maggie called Victoria again. But there was little they could do except reassure one another.

"She and Vince usually go out to the casino for dinner on Friday night," Victoria reminded her. "You know that Vince likes to play a little poker while they're there. And Louise will probably feed a few dollars into the slots. If this was serious, I'm sure they wouldn't have gone. And they sure wouldn't be staying late to play."

Victoria's reasoning was sound, but Maggie still had

trouble accepting it. Her instincts were normally trustworthy, and therefore difficult to discount.

It was late when Louise finally returned her call. Thunder was rumbling overhead, and Maggie hurried into the kitchen so she could use the cordless phone. She could see lightning flashes on the horizon, bathing the darkened room with a quirky intermittent glow. Another storm making an early appearance in the valley. This year's weather was proving as strange as the happenings in her life.

Quickly, Maggie told Louise about Detective Warner's visit.

"He was over here too, Maggie. He's just asking because Candy died unexpectedly."

"I know Andrea said they would be looking into it for that reason, but Louise, the questions he asked! He seemed particularly interested in how long you were alone with Candy, and whether or not I actually saw that she wasn't breathing when I first went into the room."

Despite the anxiety in Maggie's voice, Louise remained calm.

"Maggie, don't get excited. Vince was right here with me while I spoke to Detective Warner, and he thought it was all routine as well."

Vince, a retired lawyer, had even been a judge in Missouri before they retired to Scottsdale. But the hard lump in Maggie's stomach refused to go away.

"So you're really all right?" Maggie needed a verbal reassurance.

"Well, there is one thing."

Louise had lowered her voice, and a sudden loud thunderclap distracted Maggie.

"What did you say? I swear, the weather is so strange

this year. I don't know why we're having storms like this in the middle of May!" Another loud boom sounded. "You are on the cordless phone, aren't you?"

"Yes." Louise still kept her voice low. "I moved into the other room so that Vince won't hear. I didn't know whether or not to mention it to him."

Maggie could hear Louise take a deep breath and her stomach tightened. Outside, heavy rain began to fall, pummeling the window with staccato bursts as the wind ebbed and surged.

"What is it, Louise? Did you see something? Did you tell Detective Warner?"

"Well, yes and no." Louise paused.

The thunderstorm seemed to be moving on. Maggie heard a deep rumble, but it was farther away. Outside, the rain continued to pound against the hard ground but it too seemed to be letting up.

"I noticed something when I was giving Candy CPR. But I didn't mention it to Detective Warner." Louise hesitated, as though choosing her words carefully. "There was some redness around Candy's eyes, like she was starting to get a rash."

Maggie failed to see the importance of a rash. "It could have been a reaction to medication."

"Possibly," Louise said. "The thing is, it *could* have been petechial hemorrhaging. It's what happens in cases of strangulation or suffocation. I saw a few examples when I worked in the ER."

Maggie pulled in a breath so quickly a strange noise escaped her throat.

"The body was quite warm too, when I first found her," Louise continued. "Almost feverish. I looked it up, and that's another sign that might indicate death by asphyxiation." Louise's voice became suddenly toneless. "That might be why he was asking so many questions."

Maggie couldn't bear to hear the despair in Louise's voice. "Louise, you have to tell Vince about this, and get his advice." Maggie's mind whirled. "Asphyxiation. So she was suffocated? Like with a pillow?" Maggie felt a shiver travel down her spine. Just what she'd mentioned to Victoria.

"It's possible. It's very hard to prove someone was suffocated. And the red marking doesn't mean she *was* suffocated. There was a case in St. Louis that I remember from the newspaper. A man was arrested for killing his brother. The two men shared a house and the one was dying of cancer. They thought it was a mercy killing. But in the end, the brother's lawyer proved it was a natural death—even though there was petechial hemorrhaging."

"But suffocation is a possibility."

"It's probably just my overactive imagination." Louise laughed, but there was nothing happy about the sound.

"But it is a possibility," Maggie insisted.

Louise didn't answer for a moment. When her answer did come, her voice sounded tired.

"Yes. I think so."

Maggie wondered if Louise was scared. *She* certainly would be if the police were asking leading questions about *her* activities. Especially if she had specialized knowledge that raised questions in her own mind about the cause of death. And the reasons behind the police questions.

Maggie sighed. "It's so late. We'll talk more tomorrow."

"I don't know if I should go with you tomorrow . . ."

"Don't be silly. You're part of the Quilting Bee, and Andrea asked us all to help. We need to talk."

It was Louise's turn to sigh. "Okay. I'll see you over at the church."

131

"Come early. How about 7:30? I'll let the others know. We can talk before we leave for Candy's." Maggie's voice softened. "Take care."

The rain seemed to have stopped. At least Maggie could no longer hear it as she returned the phone to its carriage. Or perhaps her mind was just too full of murder—and plans to catch a killer—to take in something as trivial as a rain shower.

19

The Bee gathered early the next morning. Since they were all early risers, it was no inconvenience to meet at seven-thirty instead of eight forty-five. And it gave them over an hour to talk. Detective Warner had been busy, paying visits to all of the Bee members to ask about Candy and her condition in her last days. The women were buzzing with it.

Clare was thrilled. "I've never been questioned by the police before. Wasn't it exciting?"

"Much too exciting for me," Anna admitted. "Even though he just wanted to know about our visit with Candy, it still made me nervous." Anna cast a worried look toward Louise. "He was especially interested in her argument with you, Louise."

Maggie shot an uneasy glance across the frame at Louise. Since they had decided to gather in the Quilting Bee room for their talk, it seemed the most natural thing in the world to remove the sheet from the quilt frame and sit down to stitch. A fair amount of work could be done in an hour.

But before Louise had a chance to say anything, Edie responded to Anna's comment.

"I don't see why you should be nervous. You're not guilty of anything. Neither is anyone else here. It's just because Candy's death came as a surprise. Waste of taxpayer's money, if you ask me. It sounds like this detective spent the whole day going around talking to Candy's friends. Imagine what that must cost. And all for nothing."

There was a nod of agreement from Clare. "But that's why it can be exciting, Edie. Because there isn't anything there for him to discover. So I can have the experience without the stress."

"I don't know about that, Clare." Maggie cut her thread but didn't reach for the spool. Instead she turned to Anna. "He asked about Louise?"

"About the disagreement she had with Candy," Anna replied. "Yes. He was very interested in it. Called it an argument. But I told him it was just a disagreement, and that everything would have been just fine on her next visit. We all know Candy wasn't herself when we were there on Monday."

Clare sent an inquisitive look toward Maggie. "He asked me about their disagreement too. What is it you're worried about, Maggie?"

But Maggie was frowning. "Odd. He didn't say anything to me about their argument. He just asked about the day she died."

"He might not have heard about the argument yet," Clare suggested. "Oh, dear." Clare's brows drew together and her hands stilled on the quilt. "Candy better have died of natural causes. Because, if not, you're going to be in trouble, Louise. All these questions about you and Candy. It's like you're a suspect or something."

As though the meaning of her words suddenly penetrated, Clare's eyes widened and she glanced at Maggie.

"That's what you meant, isn't it?"

Maggie nodded.

Louise repeated what she'd told Maggie on the phone

the night before. "It's just a routine investigation into a sudden death. He'll go in today and write up his report and that will be the end of it."

Maggie wanted to agree with Louise. But she had an awful feeling that this would not be the end of it, that there was still a lot more to come.

As though reading her mind, Edie made a comment—one Maggie was not eager to hear.

"Bad things always happen in threes," Edie said. "If the death of Candy's friend was the first, and Candy's the second, there's bound to be one more."

Her voice trailed off, leaving them to imagine the worse.

Would it be the arrest of Louise?

Anna's tentative voice broke into the brief silence that followed Edie's pronouncement of doom.

"But I thought Candy had a stroke?"

Maggie looked over at Louise. "I think you should tell them what you told me last night."

While Maggie threaded a needle and started a new line of stitching, Louise told the others about her observation on the day of Candy's death. While most of them were familiar with petechial hemorrhaging from their television watching, further explanations were necessary, and a recounting of the story about the brothers in St. Louis. When she finished there was a deep silence.

"I think," Maggie said, breaking into the gloomy thoughts they all shared, "that we should start looking into the matter of Candy's Angel of Death."

"But we all agreed that story was ridiculous," Louise said.

"But in light of what you've seen, and the general direction of the police questioning . . ." Maggie shrugged. She pinned her needle into the quilt and folded her hands in her lap. "We have to do something."

"Maggie's right," Victoria agreed. "We can't leave this until Louise is arrested."

Clare no longer seemed to be happily excited about her police interview. She looked toward Louise, concern in her eyes.

"The only problem is that we don't know any of the people she accused."

"Well, I have met Tara," Maggie said. "It's as good a place as any to start. We talked about her the other day. She seems like a good person. The thing is, there doesn't seem to be any reason for her to kill anyone. She was quite upset to think that Candy was spreading this Angel of Death story."

Anna nodded. "It isn't the kind of thing a care center wants associated with its name."

Clare agreed. "If rumors got started, they might lose clients, even go out of business."

"So why would she do anything to make it worse?" Maggie asked.

"With Candy dead, she can't tell anyone else. The rumors stop with her."

Leave it to Edie. Her words might not be welcome, but her logic seemed faultless. Maggie frowned.

"But wouldn't her death just *feed* the rumors?"

"It would depend on how many people she already told," Victoria decided. "And we don't know that, do we?"

Maggie stood. "We knew this wouldn't be easy. And it's time for us to leave for Candy's."

"Don't worry about it." Louise stood as well, and put her arm around Maggie's shoulders. "I really appreciate what you're trying to do for me. But I still think it will turn out okay. We have to put our trust in the system."

Edie laughed, more of a snort, really. She never did think much of the "system" though Maggie didn't understand exactly why.

"I think we should keep our eyes and ears open," Edie said. She helped Clare spread the sheet over the quilt frame, then retrieved her purse from the closet. "Maybe all those people will be at the funeral. On television the police always go to the funeral to see if the killer is there."

"That's a good idea," Clare agreed.

Maggie waited to hear if she had read a book like this, but Clare had no further comment. Obviously, this was one situation that was too complicated for a book plot to illuminate.

No more satisfied about Louise's future than she had been last night, Maggie led the way out to the parking lot. There was one thing she knew for sure about the funeral though. All Candy's family would be there. And the police always started looking for suspects among the family.

20

"Oh, my."

"I thought I had a lot of fabric."

The Quilting Bee women crowded the doorway of Candy's sewing room, awed by the sheer amount of fabric and supplies therein. Housed in an extra bedroom—a large extra bedroom—of Candy's spacious home, there was a long table for cutting, a smaller one holding three sewing machines, and a wall covered with shelves. The latter held books, patterns, and plastic bins filled with supplies. The walk-in closet contained numerous bins and baskets, some filled with fabrics in coordinated colors suitable for a particular project, others overflowing with fabrics of the same color. Folded yardage the size of a bed sheet or as small as a pocket handkerchief—it was all there, every color of the rainbow, but with a preponderance of reds, blues and greens.

"Well, I'd say Candy definitely wins," Louise said in a firm voice.

The others laughed. They all recognized her reference to a bumper sticker popular among quilters: She who dies with the most fabric wins.

Maggie walked into the room, turning in a tight circle to examine the situation.

"Did Andrea say what she wanted us to do exactly?" Victoria asked.

Andrea had met them at the front of the house, handed over a key to be returned later, thanked them for their help, and rushed off to a meeting.

"She said we could have almost everything for the Senior Guild. Definitely all of the fabric." Maggie had stopped before the sewing machines, but turned toward the overflowing closet as she said this.

There were some appreciative murmurs. The fabric could make numerous quilt tops, but also doll clothes, album covers—endless items that could be sold at their Halloween Bazaar. It was a wonderful gift for the church.

"She'll want a receipt, of course," Edie said. Her lips were drawn into a thin line.

She didn't say it, but Maggie knew she was thinking that Andrea had only done it for the deduction it would make on the estate's tax bill. Maggie herself hoped that there was some sentimentality present, but she couldn't be sure. Andrea seemed to believe that emotions should be repressed. Either that, or she was making a good show of handling her mother's death efficiently. Perhaps she felt the latter attitude went with her newfound business persona.

"Doesn't Andrea want to keep any of it?" Anna's voice was sad, wondering why Andrea didn't want these things that had so defined her mother.

"She said she would like to keep the Bernina sewing machine and her mother's sewing box." Maggie glanced around. "This must be it," she said, picking up a wicker basket lined with a pretty flowered fabric and filled with sewing supplies. "She mentioned her mother's thimble and scissors particularly." Maggie rummaged through the basket checking for the desired items.

"That's nice." Anna was mollified by this sign of daughterly love. "Those are just the things she would need for a small sewing box of her own."

"I'm sure that's it," Victoria said, speaking before Edie could find some other, less altruistic motive.

"Where should we begin?" the ever-practical Louise asked.

Maggie returned the sewing basket to its place on the table and glanced around the room. "Andrea thought this was messy because she doesn't sew. But it's fairly well organized. It won't be difficult to clean up."

Louise agreed. Long shelves held clear plastic containers filled with fabric, but it was easy to see that they had been carefully sorted. Candy liked deep, vibrant colors and was especially fond of red, white and blue. So there was a preponderance of these colors, but also a fair amount of greens, golds, pinks and purples. There was one bin full of pastel thirties reproduction fabrics as well.

Clare held up a few sample blocks that were lying on top of the reproduction fabrics. There was a pink kitten, a yellow puppy, and a purple butterfly. "Do you think she was making something for the twins?"

"We should save those for Andrea," Victoria said.

"These fabrics would make a wonderful Storm at Sea quilt." Edie held up a clear plastic bin of blue cottons in various shades of light and dark. "Have we ever done one for the auction?"

"I don't think so," Maggie replied. "I prefer to do appliqué blocks, or ones like Grandmother's Fan or the Dresden Plate that combine the two."

"Me too," Victoria said. "Candy's colors are a bit bright for my taste. But they are beautiful fabrics," she added, fingering a bit of purple batik. "I wouldn't want to piece a Storm at Sea myself, though the quilting would go quickly. And I've always admired the way the finished top seems to curve and swirl when it's all made with straight geometric pieces."

"Are you volunteering to make it, Edie?" Maggie asked with a smile. They often rolled their eyes at Edie's prejudices and lack of tact, but she was a talented stitcher.

Edie was busy sorting through the blue fabrics, checking for enough lights and darks with the same color values. "I'll do it. I have those heavy plastic templates so I can cut all the pieces with the rotary cutter. I made one for my niece two years ago and it wasn't difficult." She straightened up, gesturing toward a shelf near Louise. "Hand me some of those white-on-white prints," she asked. "I'll need about three yards."

As Edie and Louise busied themselves with the white fabrics, Maggie thought she heard the front door open and close. Wondering if Andrea had forgotten something and returned, Maggie stepped outside the room, ready to greet her.

Instead, she saw Nathan escorting an attractive middle-aged woman into the house. The woman was slim and petite, her straight black hair cut so that it curved beneath her chin at the front and cleared her collar at the back. She wore a neat business suit in a burgundy red with a silk scarf tucked into the neckline and a discrete gold pin on the lapel. A thin gold watchband showed beneath her sleeve at one wrist, a thick gold bracelet at the other. She returned Maggie's curious look. Nathan, however, seemed startled. For one brief moment, Maggie wondered if she had interrupted a romantic liaison.

"Mrs. Browne. Ah . . . Maggie."

Nathan took one step forward, then stopped. It was obvious to Maggie that he was at a loss for words. She managed a polite smile.

"I hope I didn't startle you, Nathan. Andrea asked us to clean up the sewing room."

Hearing her voice, Victoria and Clare stepped out into the hall as well. Anna and Edie and even Louise peered out the sewing room door, trying to see over the heads of the others. Space was limited in the hall outside the sewing room.

Nathan's gaze drifted over the faces of all the women, finally resting on Maggie.

"The Quilting Bee." He offered them a smile, but it rode on the wave of a quiet sigh, spoiling the intent. "I'd forgotten you were coming. I thought the house would be empty."

As though suddenly recognizing his duty as host—or perhaps realizing how they might interpret his last comment—Nathan gestured toward his companion. "This is Amy Wong. She's with Dream Properties."

Maggie could almost hear an "ahh" issuing from the women behind her. She didn't have to turn to know that Edie and Anna would look slightly disapproving. Well, in Edie's case, perhaps extremely disapproving. Louise and Clare would be digesting this information with interest, and Victoria's eyes would be sad.

Maggie offered her hand. "How nice to meet you, Amy."

The other woman had a firm grip and a pleasant smile. Maggie liked her.

"I'm . . ."

The sound of a door opening further down the hall prevented Amy from finishing what she'd begun.

By now, everyone had managed to squeeze out into the hall. They all turned.

Two doors down—Maggie thought the room between was probably the bathroom—the door opened inward revealing a disheveled Stephanie, her hand held to her mouth and covering a wide yawn.

"What's going on out here? Don't you know it's the weekend? Time to sleep in."

The surprise of the earlier encounter was nothing to everyone's amazement now. The Bee women had believed themselves alone in the house. Nathan thought the house was empty. And Stephanie had been there all along.

Maggie didn't think she'd ever seen a person's mouth drop open. She'd often read of this phenomenon in fiction, of course, but now she saw it in actuality. Nathan was staring at his sister, his lips parted. He seemed to realize it at about the same time Maggie noticed. He snapped his mouth closed, his lips meeting in a tight, thin line.

"Stephanie." Nathan took a step forward. "What are you doing here?"

Maggie could hear the irritation in his voice. His shoulders were tense, his neck jutting forward. She noticed that he clenched and unclenched his near hand.

Stephanie offered her brother a smile filled with sugar.

"It was Daddy's house, so now it will be ours. And it's just sitting here empty while Kendall and I were squeezed into that awful one bedroom apartment. I just know Daddy would have wanted us to move in." Her voice trailed off and she smiled at all the women gathered in the hall.

Maggie had to smile back. Stephanie sure knew how to play up to a man. There was something of the southern belle about her, and the hint of a drawl in her silky voice. Maggie wondered where she'd been living these last few years. Maggie's thought that Stephanie must have been in the south was affirmed by the voice that came from the room behind her.

"Is it time to get up?"

The voice sounded young, and had a very definite twang. Texas, maybe. It was followed by the emergence of a young boy, perhaps eight, dressed in cotton pajamas printed with cowboys riding bucking broncos. Blinking in surprise, he looked around the crowded hallway; his face broke into a huge grin when he saw Nathan.

"Hey, Uncle Nathan. Is cousin Caitlin with you?"

His eager face moved around the group again. Maggie decided he must have a pleasant relationship with his young cousin.

"Sorry, Kenny, she's at home with her Mom."

Nathan smiled at his nephew, and his voice was kind, but Maggie had a feeling he was still irritated at his sister.

"So what are y'all doing out here?" Stephanie asked.

She patted her right hand over her hip, then seemed to realize she was dressed only in a long oversized T-shirt. Her sigh made Maggie realize she was looking for a cigarette, and had just found herself with no pocket and no pack.

When Nathan declined to answer right away, Maggie spoke.

"Andrea asked us to come over and clean up Candy's sewing room. She's donating most of the supplies to the church for the Quilting Bee and the Senior Guild."

Stephanie glanced around again, seemed to place them. "Oh, yes. The quilting ladies. Candy always talked about y'all." She ran her fingers through her hair, pushing it off her forehead. Then she nodded. "Nice to see y'all again. I think we met last year when I came for the Halloween Bazaar. Kenny really enjoyed it."

Beside her, the little boy nodded enthusiastically, but hung back behind his mother. He was a darling child, but shy, Maggie thought. Her grandsons would have begun regaling them with accounts of the Bazaar and all the things they'd done there.

"Well, I'll just go change and maybe I can help you out. I didn't want to move into Candy's room. It didn't seem right somehow, with her not even buried yet. So Kenny and I are both camping out in the guest room. It'll be nice to have another room to use." She put her hand on her son's head, ruffling his sandy hair. "You might have your own room soon, hon. What do you think of that?"

"Great!" Kenny's smile showed a missing tooth at the front.

As he and his mother disappeared into the room behind them, the group in the hall shifted. The Bee women moved back into the sewing room, but Maggie lingered in the doorway. She was anxious to see what Nathan was going to do about Amy. She didn't have long to wait.

Amy turned to Nathan, impatience in every line of her slim body. "I thought you said you were anxious to sell this place?"

She kept her voice low, though some anger came through. Probably upset about wasting her time, Maggie thought. Someone who dressed like Amy Wong must be a very successful realtor. She would not be happy about losing an entire weekend morning.

"I am," Nathan insisted.

He, too, kept his voice down. But Maggie could still hear the irritation. Anger on his side too, she thought.

"I told you my stepmother just died. This house comes to both my sister and I. She doesn't have the money to buy out my share, so we'll have to sell it. I don't know what kind of game she's playing, but I'll be talking to her about it."

"When you do, you know where to find me. Make sure

you both agree next time."

Amy turned on her stylish heel and walked out. Maggie couldn't help thinking that she probably wanted to slam the door behind her. She was too well bred to do so, of course. Whatever her secret desires, the door closed with a quiet wheeze. Just as it did, Stephanie emerged from the other bedroom. She was dressed in denim shorts and a faded T-shirt that read "Don't Mess With Texas." There was no cigarette in her hand, but the reek of tobacco smoke floated into the hall with her.

"So, what can I do to help?"

21

"Why Detective Warner!"

Maggie stared at the man standing on her doorstep, almost forgetting to invite him in. Stymied by his presence, all she could do was wonder why he was there!

"Hello, Mrs. Browne. I'm sorry to bother you again, but I have a few more questions."

"Ah, certainly." Maggie stood aside and gestured him in. "Could I offer you some iced tea?"

To her surprise, Detective Warner agreed to a glass of tea and she went into the kitchen to get it.

Once they were settled in the living room with their glasses of tea, Maggie looked to the detective. Her eyes were questioning.

"I wanted to ask you about your earlier visit to the Palo Verde Care Center," Detective Warner began. He sipped at his tea while he consulted his notebook. "I believe you visited with the rest of your quilting group on Monday afternoon."

"Yes. We took Candy a lap quilt we'd made."

To Maggie's surprise, Detective Warner smiled.

"Very nice of you."

Maggie acknowledged this with a half-hearted smile of her own. He was being very polite and every bit the gentleman, but she wasn't sure she trusted him. She was still suspicious of the questions he'd asked yesterday, still sure he suspected foul play and was focused on Louise as prime suspect.

"Could you describe your visit with Mrs. Breckner on Monday please?"

Maggie eyed him for a moment then plunged into a recounting of their visit with Candy. It wasn't until she got to the part about Candy yelling at Louise that Maggie began to falter. If her suspicions were true, the argument with Louise would not look good. But she had to tell him about it; he already knew. In fact, Maggie wondered why he'd even bothered coming back for her version. Looking for contradictions in their stories, perhaps?

When she'd finished, Detective Warner asked about Louise. As she'd suspected he would—but hoped he would not.

"So your friend Louise did not make up with Mrs. Breckner that day?"

"No. Candy was so worked up, we suggested she wait until later. That's why Louise was there on Thursday. When Victoria and I visited Candy on Wednesday, we told her that Louise would come the next day. She was fine with it. Didn't say a thing about Louise or about what happened Monday, just nodded."

"And how did Louise feel about going over?"

"Louise had been very upset about the whole thing. She was anxious to make up with Candy. She wanted to do it on Monday, but Candy was so unlike her regular self. It came as such a surprise to us, the way she was acting."

"About Louise, you mean?"

"No, about everything. She wanted to go home, but anyone could see she would never be able to manage on her own at home. And then when she mentioned this Angel of

Death thing . . . We talked about it the next day. We wondered if she was on some kind of medication that was making her paranoid."

"Did Mrs. Breckner lose her temper often?"

Maggie pursed her lips as she thought this over. "Now and then. Candy was the emotional type. She could lose her temper quickly, but then she got over it quickly, too. None of us thought anything of that blowup with Louise, except for feeling bad about the whole thing. And with her in the care center, it was harder for her to make up with Louise."

Detective Warner nodded. "Your friend, Louise. She's a registered nurse?"

It was Maggie's turn to nod.

"Have you ever seen her administer CPR before?"

Maggie tried to decide if this was an incriminating question. But if it was she couldn't see how.

"Everyone at St. Rose's—at both the church and the Senior Guild—knows that Louise is an RN. So if someone has a problem—at the Guild meetings or at church while she's there—they'll call her."

Maggie stopped, but she noticed that Detective Warner continued to look expectant. She realized why when he addressed her again.

"So have you? Seen her administer CPR?"

"Oh." Maggie realized she had not answered his original question. Though she did feel she had addressed the issue. She could hear her dear husband saying, "women can never give a simple yes or no answer." Harry, though, usually smiled when he said it. Detective Warner just watched her with a somber expression on his face. Not for the first time she thought that he would make an excellent poker player.

"I have seen Louise help out when someone has collapsed. I remember one incident at the church when she did

CPR. It was last year some time, in the morning when we're all there working on the Senior Guild projects. Jack Osborn thought he was having a heart attack. Someone dialed 911, and someone else called Louise. His heart stopped before the paramedics arrived, and she started CPR. The paramedics were very praiseworthy. They said she saved his life. Jack sent her a beautiful bouquet of flowers when he recovered."

Maggie watched Detective Warner but he didn't nod or say anything. He did jot something down in his notebook. Jack Osborn's name she suspected.

"So, was that the only time?"

Maggie couldn't imagine where he was heading with his questions. How many times does anyone get to save another's life? Surely doctors and nurses were given the opportunity more than the average citizen, but still . . .

"That's the only time that I was there. I heard that she helped a woman who went into labor during mass one time. But that didn't involve CPR of course."

"Did the woman have the baby during the service?"

Maggie smiled. "Almost. Apparently it was her first baby and while she was uncomfortable that morning she didn't realize she was actually in labor. So she came to mass— alone too. Her husband wasn't Catholic and he stayed home. The way I heard it later, the person who called him thought she'd awakened him."

Maggie stopped long enough to take a sip of her tea. This was a lovely story and reflected well on Louise.

"Anyway, halfway through mass, her water broke and her contractions got pretty bad. It was the mass Louise was attending, and she went over when they asked if there were any doctors in the house. There was one doctor there, a dermatologist," she added with a smile. "So Louise was a big help. She has three children of her own, you know. That baby was anxious to enter the world, and wasn't about to wait for the paramedics to get there. It was a little boy and they gave him the middle name Louis in her honor."

Detective Warner seemed to reflect on this for a moment, and once again Maggie's imagination ran wild. She'd give anything to know what the man was thinking.

But Maggie wasn't to know. He closed his notebook, finished off his last bit of tea, thanked her and left.

Maggie rushed to the phone and called Victoria. She'd barely said hello when Victoria had to excuse herself to answer the door. When she returned to say she would have to call Maggie back later, Maggie asked if Detective Warner was her caller.

"Why, yes."

"He just left here. Call me back when he's gone."

It took almost half an hour, during which Maggie worked at an appliqué block in fits and starts. When Victoria finally called, Maggie was eager to know what Detective Warner had asked her.

"He asked about my visits with Candy," Victoria told her. "I'd already told him about them the last time he was here, but he asked again. Then he asked if I'd ever seen Louise give anyone CPR. Isn't that strange?"

"That's what he asked me about too. I'm not sure yet what to make of it, but one thing for sure, it doesn't make me feel good. He's got his eye on Louise and it seems too much is going on here for just a natural death. Like Edie said, it's taxpayer money he's spending, going around and asking all these questions."

"But if she was murdered, how was it done? How could someone suffocate her in her bed, there in that busy place?"

"I don't know. But I think it's time we start considering the possibilities."

22

"Louise?"

Maggie was back on the telephone. She and Victoria had talked around and around the problem, but they had not reached any conclusions. There was too much they didn't know. Including the cause of death.

"Detective Warner was here again," Maggie told Louise. "Did he call on you too?"

"No. But then Vince and I have been out. We just got back."

"He saw Victoria too. And he's asking the strangest questions."

"What do you mean, strange?"

"He wanted to know if I'd ever seen you administer CPR. He asked Victoria the same thing."

There was no comment from Louise, but Maggie knew she was thinking.

"Do you have any idea what he might be trying to get at?"

"No."

Maggie heard a sigh.

"I guess it's time I told Vince everything."

"You haven't told him about the rash you saw?"

"No." Louise sounded tired. "Maybe I'm just kidding myself, Maggie. I don't want to believe Candy didn't die a natural death. And I really don't want to believe I could be a suspect in a murder investigation."

Maggie could understand that.

"That's only natural, Louise."

"Once I tell Vince, it will all be real. I won't be able to pretend the police are doing a normal inquiry into a sudden death. Vince will start to suspect every question, probably won't let me talk to them at all."

"Maybe that's just as well. I'm scared for you, Louise. I don't know what kind of evidence the police have, but I don't like the questions they're asking. Everything seems directed toward where you were and what you did."

There was a reluctant chuckle from Louise. "And the funny thing is, I didn't do anything."

But Maggie didn't see any humor in the situation.

"Louise, how long would it take to suffocate a person?"

Maggie had been thinking about this. If someone *had* killed Candy by holding a pillow over her head, it would have to be done quickly. There were too many people around at the care center for him (or her, she reminded herself) to take a long time about it. A staff member or another patient could easily walk in at any time. And Louise had said the body was very warm when she started CPR.

"Maggie, I'm afraid I don't really know."

"Can you guess? I'm trying to work out if it could be done, but I don't have enough information."

"Well . . ."

Maggie could picture Louise at the other end of the phone line. She would be thinking, her eyes staring, unfocused. She'd probably rolled her lips inward and tipped her chin up.

"Candy was a small woman," she began, "and weak from the accident. Those casts would have made it difficult for her to fight off a strong person. I don't think it would take too long."

The thought of how quickly death could arrive made Maggie's stomach clench. "I told Detective Warner that you might have been alone with Candy for two minutes. No more than that."

"I don't know, Maggie. That seems like a very short time, but I'm certainly no expert."

Louise sounded weary, and Maggie was sympathetic.

"I'm sorry to bring all this up, Louise, but I just wish I knew what he was trying to get at today."

Two minutes later, Maggie was still thinking about that as she disconnected the call. She knew Detective Warner was after something. Something specific, and it had to do with Louise administering CPR. Could he think she didn't know how to do it properly? That didn't seem to make any sense. But what else was there?

23

"Hey, Ma."

Maggie's eldest son called to her as she exited the kitchen with a new pot of coffee.

The Browne family Sunday brunch was in full swing, the back yard picnic tables full of food and people. When Maggie and her Harry were raising their family, Sundays meant a long drive down to St. Rose for the morning mass. So Maggie always made a special brunch for the family when they returned. It had become a family tradition, fondly remembered by all the boys.

Now the family was scattered throughout Scottsdale, and there were churches closer to their homes. But most of them still attended St. Rose, and all were always welcome back to the ranch for the Sunday brunch, now hosted by Hal and his wife Sara. But they never could convince Maggie to just sit and enjoy the meal.

Hal accepted another cup of coffee from his mother, then gave her a mischievous smile.

"What are you and your detectives working on these days?"

Michael frowned but the others laughed. They enjoyed teasing Maggie about being their very own Miss Marple. A younger version, of course.

Maggie looked over at Michael before answering. Her frown equaled his.

"Well, I told Michael about this on Monday . . ."

"Not that Angel of Death thing," Michael muttered.

"Angel of Death?"

There were interested murmurs from around the table.

"There was a bit on that news program last week about an Angel of Death," Sara said. "A nurse in California was killing his patients because he felt their lives were being needlessly prolonged."

Maggie turned toward her daughter-in-law. "That was probably the program that Candy and her friend saw at the care center."

"Yes," Michael agreed, "and it gave them ideas. They probably thought it would make their lives more interesting if they suspected there was someone like that at their facility."

"Here? In Scottsdale?" Merrie asked.

All the adult attention now focused on Maggie and her story as she told them about Candy and her fears and premonitions.

"Then she died so suddenly," Maggie concluded. She paused long enough to take a sip of cooling coffee from her mug. "And now a police detective—a *homicide* detective," she added, with a distinctive look toward Michael, "has been to visit all the Bee members, asking questions."

Michael dismissed this. "That's normal procedure in any unexpected death, Ma."

"Still, it has us all wondering if there may be something to her fears. It seems far-fetched, but we all saw her just beforehand, and she was looking so well." Maggie looked grim. "I'm especially concerned about the questions that detective is asking. It sounds to me like he suspects an unnatural death and that he's focused on Louise as his prime suspect."

"Not Louise!" Merrie seemed shocked to hear this. Sara, sitting beside her seemed equally amazed.

Maggie nodded. "He's asked everyone about a disagreement she had with Candy when we visited on Monday. Louise told her she was letting her imagination run away with her, thinking there was an Angel of Death in the building. And Candy got very upset and screamed at her. But she wasn't herself that day, and it really was nothing."

"He thinks Louise would kill someone because she yelled at her a few days earlier?" Sara's lips twitched before spreading in a smile.

But Maggie didn't see any humor in the situation. "He asked me very particularly how long she was alone in the room with Candy the day we discovered her body. And if I actually saw that Candy wasn't breathing when I walked in. And he wanted to know if I noticed the condition of the room—whether the bed and bedding was neat or mussed, or what."

"Oh, my."

Maggie nodded toward Merrie. She at least saw the implication.

"And yesterday he asked if I'd ever seen her perform CPR on anyone. I thought that a rather strange question. He asked Victoria the same thing."

"Oh, dear."

Maggie turned toward Sara. "What is it?"

"There was a follow-up on that Angel of Death story. I saw it the other night. Another case, this one in Ohio. A woman there is accused of killing several patients by injecting them with a substance that puts them into cardiac arrest. Then she would attempt to save them. And she did save many of them, but not all. The prosecutor is arguing that she did it for the glory of being a hero when she saved them. She was also supposed to be trying to impress one of the male nurses who she was dating."

"I doubt Louise is dating a nurse at Palo Verde," Michael joked. But his attempt at humor fell flat.

"Doesn't sound good for Louise," Merrie said.

"That's just what I've been trying to tell her. I think she's starting to get worried." Maggie looked toward Michael, debating the wisdom of releasing her latest information. "Louise told me she saw some signs that Candy may not have died of natural causes."

"What?" Michael was not happy. "Did you tell Detective Warner about this?"

Maggie shook her head. "I didn't find out until after I spoke to him."

"What did she see?" Frank asked. Being a veterinarian, he was the closest thing to a medical person in the family.

"Well, she said there was a rash around her eyes that could be petechial hemorrhaging."

At curious glances from a few of the others, Michael spoke. "They're little pin-point hemorrhages that appear when a person dies of asphyxiation. Usually around the eyes and mouth."

"She said the body was very warm when she discovered it too. I guess that's another sign of asphyxiation."

There was a moment of silence as they digested this information.

"Isn't Louise's husband a lawyer?" Sara asked.

Maggie nodded. "And a retired judge. She said he's been there with her when she's been questioned, but so far he doesn't see any problems."

"I agree with him," Michael said. "It's routine procedure to check into sudden deaths. That doesn't mean it wasn't a natural death. Despite Louise's observations."

"Louise said that too." Maggie was glad to give him that.

"She said that even if it was petechial hemorrhaging she saw, it doesn't mean death wasn't due to natural causes. She mentioned a case she remembered in St. Louis."

Maggie paused a moment while she looked at her children, all listening intently. "But it's the nature of the questions Detective Warner is asking that I find troubling."

Maggie looked to Michael, but he wasn't about to encourage her.

"She was in a hospital, Ma. She was old."

"It was a convalescent home," Maggie corrected him. "There's a big difference between that and a hospital. The people aren't that sick in a convalescent home."

She turned toward Michael, spearing him with a stern "mother" look. "And she was a year younger than I am."

Sara hooted with laughter, and the others joined in. Michael was in trouble now, and they knew it. Michael, looking sheepish, mumbled an apology and quickly headed toward the kitchen on some desperate errand.

Maggie turned to Bobby. "By the way, I meant to tell you on the phone the other night and forgot . . . The head nurse over at the convalescent home where Candy was staying is an old school friend of yours. Tara McClintock. Her last name is Dillion now."

Bobby nodded his recognition of the name. "Sure, I remember her. Haven't seen her since the ten year reunion."

Maggie smiled at Merrie. "Tara is expecting her first child too."

Merrie glanced at her husband. "Did I meet her?"

"Yeah, sure. And Andrea, too, at the reunion. I run into Andrea now and then. You know, running into the drug store or passing through the grocery store. But not so often lately. I suppose she's a lot busier now that she has that gift shop."

He turned toward his mother. "I was surprised when you called and told me that Mrs. Breckner died. Last time I saw Andrea she was saying how much her mother enjoyed the Senior Guild at church." Bobby smiled at his mother. "She knows you're involved too, so I guess that's why she mentioned it."

"We were over at Candy's yesterday," Maggie told them. "Andrea asked us to help clean up her mother's sewing room. She offered to let us have her supplies for the Senior Guild."

Michael, just back from the house with a pitcher of iced tea, frowned, perhaps trying to find some ulterior motive behind his mother's getting involved with cleaning up Candy's house.

"That's real nice for you, Ma," Hal said.

"We're very happy with what we'll be getting. You wouldn't believe what Candy had stocked away in her sewing room."

Maggie's sons laughed.

"I would," Hal said.

"Me, too," Bobby echoed. "Remember, we helped you move from here to your condo." His brothers all nodded.

"Man, I never saw so many boxes of fabric," Frank agreed.

"Well, okay, so you understand." Maggie grinned at her boys. "But Candy had more than any of us. And that's saying a lot."

"Maybe she used shopping and sewing to keep her mind off her being all alone," Sara suggested.

Maggie nodded at her daughter-in-law. How wise she already was. "That might be. Once your children are grown and your husband is gone, you have to fill the time somehow. And Candy lost two husbands."

"And Andrea is so busy with her store."

"She also has four-year-old twins," Maggie told them.

"What about the stepchildren?" Bobby asked.

"They were both there yesterday. Nathan and Stephanie." Maggie sighed. "We met at the church and carpooled over to the house. Andrea met us outside with the key then hurried off to a meeting of some kind. We'd barely started when Nathan came in. With a realtor." Maggie shook her head, her lips pulled into a tight line. "Some of the others think it's unseemly the way Nathan is so anxious to sell the house."

Hal shrugged. "Everyone knows his business is in trouble. He spent a lot on a parcel of land in North Scottsdale. Then he had to reduce the number of houses he planned to put up. Even with that, he's still battling with the zoning people and the neighbors. What he thought would be a good investment with a quick turnaround is taking a long time and costing a lot of money."

Michael nodded. "I've heard about it too. The neighbors are up in arms over it. The existing lots out there are five to ten acres with horse privileges. Nathan wants to build a golf course with some of the lots less than an acre. The people out there want to keep the western rural nature of the neighborhood and are determined to keep the density low. And they're adamantly opposed to a golf course. That's why it's taking so long. They show up in force at every zoning and city council meeting. The vote has been postponed several times."

"I've been following the story in the paper," Maggie said. "I figured he wanted a quick sale for that reason. But now his sister Stephanie has moved into the house. And she's decided she'd rather live there than sell."

"Won't she have to sell?" Bobby asked. "Or does she

have enough money to buy his half outright?"

Maggie shook her head. "I don't think she has any money at all. Stephanie helped us—after our talking woke her up. Nathan didn't know she'd moved in, and I don't think he's very happy about it. She's back in town after a divorce. I don't think it was a friendly one either."

"Don't you have to probate the will before you can sell off property?" Merrie looked over to Hal.

"You understand this isn't my area of expertise . . ."

His brothers laughed. They were used to Hal's "lawyer mindset" and his qualifications to statements.

"He can sell the house and put the money into the estate. His sister would get her share when they settle."

"Candy's house should be worth a lot," Bobby said. "It's in a nice part of town, and the houses there have been increasing in value steadily over the years. Half of that should be enough for Stephanie to get a place of her own."

"True," Hal said. "But you don't know if there's a mortgage outstanding, and there would be taxes. Plus commissions for the realtor, maybe fees for an estate lawyer."

"You aren't trying to say that you think Nathan or Stephanie had something to do with their stepmother's death?" Sara looked stricken at even the thought.

"No." Maggie's reply came quickly. "I'm just considering motives if she was killed. I know Louise didn't do it. And until she died, I didn't think much of that Angel of Death business."

"Thank goodness," Michael muttered.

Maggie glanced at her youngest son. He might think she didn't hear him, but there was nothing wrong with her ears.

"I told Detective Warner about Candy's suspicions. And who she named."

"Great," Michael said. "He'll take it from there."

Maggie knew what was implied. *So you can leave it be.* She turned toward Michael.

But before Maggie could speak, Sara rose from the table. "Come on, girls," she said, taking Maggie by the arm and urging her to rise. "Let's let the guys clean up. I want you to see the rose garden, Ma. It's just beautiful right now."

Maggie was glad of the suggestion. She had planted the rose garden herself many years ago and she was happy that Sara was enthusiastic in its upkeep. There was something peaceful about the beautiful blooming plants, and the delicate scent was soothing to the spirit. It was just what Maggie needed right now. Perhaps Sara would let her cut some blossoms to take home. A bit of natural aromatherapy might be just what she needed.

Amid a storm of good-natured protests from the men, Maggie and her daughters-in-law strolled across the lawn, murder temporarily forgotten.

24

"It was a lovely service." Anna dabbed at her eyes with a lace-edged handkerchief.

The Quilting Bee women stood together on the patio of Andrea's house. They had joined a large number of others, many of them Senior Guild members, at the open house held there after Candy's funeral. Candy had been active in many areas of the church, and her funeral had filled St. Rose to capacity. Luckily, not everyone had continued on to the graveyard and then to Andrea's.

"The music was beautiful," Victoria said. "I didn't know Candy sang in the choir."

The nine o'clock mass choir had offered to perform at the funeral in honor of their former colleague, and they had outdone themselves. Tears flowed freely during the beautiful, stirring hymns; there wasn't a dry eye in the church at the end of the Ave Maria.

"It was quite a few years ago, before she joined the Senior Guild," Clare told her. "She said she didn't want to come back in the evening for choir practice when she was spending all morning at the church."

"It's where she met Ken," Edie added. "She probably didn't want to continue after he died."

Clare, who seemed to know Candy best, didn't contradict her. Maggie nodded a silent agreement. Some widows enjoyed continuing the activities they had enjoyed with their husbands. Some couldn't face the memories.

Louise remained silent, her head turned toward the oasis created by the swimming pool.

Maggie put her empty punch cup on a table and joined Louise. She too looked out over the backyard. A free form pool with pebbled lining filled half of the fenced-in area. Water tumbled over large boulders piled up at the far end, just inside the block fence. Small plants added a touch of green amid the rocks, and lush palms and banana plants created the illusion of a rain forest pond. The wide leaves of the banana contrasted nicely with the stiff spikes of the palms and the clusters of bird of paradise blooming beneath it. There was even a grouping of bamboo plants tucked into the corner where the fence created a right angle.

The sound of the waterfall was soothing, as were the softly stirring leaves of the palms and bamboo. Misters along the edges of the patio and arcade roofs kept them comfortable in the warming day. Maggie wasn't surprised that so many of the guests had been drawn outside.

"Lovely, isn't it?" Maggie drew up beside Louise, her gaze still fixed on the greenery before them. "But imagine the work to keep the pool water clean with all those palms and especially that bamboo around it."

Louise smiled. "I hadn't thought about it, but you're right. We just have two palms near ours and they contribute a lot of trash to the water. That bamboo must be awful."

Edie, standing nearby and overhearing their comments, moved closer. "I'm sure they have a yard man. And a pool man."

Maggie heard what she left unsaid. "With a house like this." And she agreed of course. Andrea's house was located in a gated community in northern Scottsdale. It was large and *House Beautiful* perfect. Maggie found it hard to imagine four-year-old twins actually living in it.

Edie was still staring at the lovely pool. "Humph! A rain forest in the desert. It's a crime the water they must waste keeping all this green."

"It is beautiful though, Edie, you have to admit that," Louise said.

Grudgingly, Edie did. "But desert plants can be just as beautiful," she insisted.

"No argument from me there," Maggie said. She loved the desert and all its various and unique plants. And while this yard was beautiful and the water soothing to the spirit, she could sympathize with Edie's viewpoint. Beauty came in various guises, and another setting for the pool could have been equally lovely.

"Ladies . . ."

Andrea walked up to the Quilting Bee members, her arm slung through Bobby's. Maggie noticed that she had circles under her eyes, a condition not unexpected at your mother's funeral. But she smiled at the gathered women, a sincere smile of thanks.

"It's so nice to see Bobby again," she told Maggie. "We old friends just don't seem to find the time for each other any more. It's a shame it has to be a sad occasion like this to bring us together again."

Bobby nodded toward his mother and her friends, then squeezed Andrea's hand. "Let me move on so that you can talk to Ma and her friends. I know they were all close to your mother."

He turned toward Maggie. "Would you like a ride home, Ma?"

Maggie had ridden to the church with Victoria, and they had brought Anna and Edie along with them to the graveyard and the reception. Victoria would have company on the long drive back to the church, and she was anxious to see what Bobby thought of today's Andrea. So she accepted his offer and he moved off toward a group of young people.

Andrea watched him leave, all the while exchanging the usual post-funeral small talk about the deceased with the Bee women. Then she became silent. She looked uneasy, her eyes darting from one to another of the Quilting Bee ladies.

"I wonder if I could impose on you all." She laughed—a high-pitched, nervous sound. "Again. Thank you for your work on Mother's sewing room, by the way. I hope her fabrics and things will be useful for you."

"We'll make some beautiful quilts with what you gave us," Edie told her.

"Yes," Clare agreed. "It's a nice legacy for Candy."

"What else can we help with?" Maggie inquired.

Andrea's eyes moved down toward her feet, then back up again. Her eyes looked briefly into Maggie's, then shifted rapidly among the others.

"I would really appreciate it if you wouldn't tell anyone about Mother and that Angel of Death obsession of hers," she finally said. "It makes it look like she was crazy," she added with a grimace.

Maggie thought it interesting that Andrea was no longer meeting their eyes. Did she realize that Maggie was the one who had told the police about the Angel of Death?

"We already spoke to the police about it," Anna answered.

Andrea frowned. "Well, there's nothing that can be done about that. And I guess the police should know. But I was thinking more of people in general." Her hand gestured outward, encompassing the crowd on the patio and in the yard. "It would be nice if not everyone at the church knew about that Angel of Death thing. It's not as if she was killed by an Angel of Death after all. That story was patently ridiculous."

Before any of the Bee women could comment, Tara detached herself from the group of young mourners and approached them.

Maggie gave her a hug.

Andrea shook her hand. "How nice of you to come."

Maggie approved of the words, yet she wished Andrea could say them with more feeling. The young woman was apparently the polar opposite of her emotional mother. Though it was possible that she was moving through the funeral on autopilot, trying to stay detached to get through it. Maggie liked that explanation best.

She returned her attention to the two young women just in time to hear Tara's reply to Andrea's platitude.

"I try to attend the funeral of anyone who dies at Palo Verde."

Maggie noted Andrea's approving nod, even as she made her excuses and moved toward the next group of mourners.

"Does it happen often?"

Clare's question to Tara caught Maggie's attention. She turned away from Andrea and back toward the other woman. Maggie noticed that Tara shifted her weight from one foot to the other, like someone anxious to move on. But she did answer.

"Not often. But of course it does happen. Most of our patients are elderly."

"Candy said something about a friend of hers who died," Maggie said. "Rhonda, I believe. There may have been another she mentioned as well."

"Jane," Clare contributed. "Jane Madison."

"Yes, that's right," Maggie said. "Jane lived near the church and we all knew her from the Bazaar. Their deaths were the reasons she gave for thinking there was an Angel of Death."

Tara sighed. "I remember that she was very upset about Rhonda's death."

"Candy said she was in the early stages of Alzheimer's. Did she really have to be in a care facility?"

Tara's eyes drifted to the group of young people and back again. "Her family thought it best. She lived alone and had no relatives here in the valley. She had to take medication for other medical problems—they were worried that she wouldn't remember to take it. That she wouldn't eat properly. There were a lot of factors."

"I see." Maggie wondered if she should ask how she died. But she thought Tara would probably not reply since she had phrased her previous answer so carefully. Maggie realized that she was protecting her client's privacy. "Candy said Rhonda was the one who first suspected an Angel of Death."

Tara raised her brows. "Now that's interesting."

25

But Maggie was not to learn why Tara found it so interesting that Rhonda had first conceived the notion of an Angel of Death. A raised voice coming from the arcade doors distracted them—and the rest of the gathering. Conversation in the yard came to a standstill and all eyes turned toward the house to see who might be shouting so indiscriminately at a funeral reception.

But Andrea apparently knew exactly who it was. With a sigh, she left the couple she was speaking to and hurried toward the door. Maggie saw her take the arm of a tall, sandy-haired man and lead him toward the kitchen. Nathan was there too, trying to help, but being shaken off by the other man. They saw Andrea's head tip earnestly forward as she spoke. Her mouth was close to his ear, and not a whisper traveled to the women in the yard. When Andrea finally pulled her head back, her companion looked like a pouting child, but he did follow her, taking a moment to address the still silent group of mourners.

"Sorry, folks. Didn't mean any disrespect," he announced.

Nathan tried to follow as the couple disappeared into the house, but once again the other man brushed him aside. Nathan, turning toward the table where his wife sat, noted the attention still fixed on him and shrugged elaborately.

Then, with a small smile, he joined his wife on the patio, placing a hand on her shoulder and bending to say a few words to her.

The Quilting Bee women watched the whole episode with interest.

"Wasn't that Andrea's husband?" Victoria asked.

"Sure was," Maggie said. "I wonder what that was all about."

Tara shook her head. "All Candy's relatives were . . ." She paused.

"Disruptive?" Maggie supplied.

Tara shrugged, apparently accepting the word but unwilling to use it herself. "I liked Candy. When her kids weren't around she was a nice woman."

"It's hard for us to accept that she's gone," Anna admitted.

"We'd just visited with her . . ." Clare explained.

Victoria nodded. "Except for that strange story about an Angel of Death, she seemed so healthy."

Tara frowned. "I thought so too. But death can come quickly, from strokes or blood clots. Clots are common after automobile accidents. The patient seems quite normal, then suddenly, he or she is dead, with no warning."

Maggie noticed Louise nod. Maggie was worried about Louise. It wasn't like her to be so introspective. But meanwhile, Clare had seized on Tara's last statement.

"So you were surprised too. About Candy's death, I mean."

"Have the police questioned you about it?" Maggie asked.

Tara nodded. "Yes, but that's routine in any sudden death." Tara looked around her at the Bee women. The corners of her lips turned downward, the beginning of a frown. "You aren't thinking there is an Angel of Death!"

"No, no," Maggie hastened to reassure her. "It's just that a police detective has been questioning us all. And we're trying to understand what might have happened." No use telling her how she felt they were aiming their questions at Louise. Tara was touchy about the Angel of Death subject.

Victoria nodded. "Candy was in quite a state when we visited on Monday."

"Very emotional, and not really herself," Clare added.

Tara's expression was still friendly, but her voice became neutral. "As I said, Candy's family's visits had an unusual effect on her. The Palo Verde Care Center is an excellent facility. Why don't you come out and see for yourselves." Her eyes roamed over the group, extending the invitation to them all. "In fact, Candy had been showing off her quilt blocks and some of the others were very interested in her work. Perhaps you would be able to do a demonstration, or offer a lesson."

Maggie was immediately interested. She could see that Clare was as well. This was the perfect opportunity for them to learn more about the care center. And about Joseph and the gardener.

Anxious not to lose such an excellent opportunity, Maggie arranged with Tara to visit the care center the following afternoon.

"We should do it right away, while there's an interest," Maggie suggested. "I'm sure there's a turnover rate there, as people get better and return to their homes."

Tara assured them that the following afternoon would be fine, and announced that she really had to get over to the center. As she walked toward the house to leave, Andrea and her husband came back out, side by side. Edie saw them and clicked her tongue.

"What a pair. She barely mentions losing her mother. Just fusses about what a busy time it is at work. And him shouting like that, disrupting the funeral." One side of Edie's mouth turned down and her shoulders stiffened.

"I think he had too much to drink," Louise said.

If possible, Edie looked even more disapproving.

"But they aren't serving liquor." Anna's voice expressed her surprise at Louise's conclusion.

"It's his house, though," Maggie told her. "And it would explain his behavior." Her expression turned thoughtful.

"It's darn unnatural," Edie insisted. "Not as if it's his mother."

"I think it's a combination of things, with Andrea at least," Victoria said. "Her mother's death, plus the stress of owning her own business." Her voice softened. "And perhaps a difficult marriage."

"The poor dear." Anna was instantly sympathetic. "Do you think her husband has a drinking problem?"

Louise shrugged. "Hard to tell. Something as major as a parent dying can push a person toward drink."

"But, like Edie said, it's not his mother," Anna pointed out. "And I didn't think they were close. It might be easier to understand if Nathan was drunk and shouting."

"Oh, but Candy wasn't his mother. He was a grown man when Candy married his father," Clare reminded her. "And he's so anxious to sell her house," Clare added, her voice sad. "Makes you think he might not be so upset, doesn't it?"

A gleam appeared in Clare's eye that Maggie recognized. It was "I read in this book" time.

"You know," Clare said, "I read this book once where the stepson killed his father's second wife—poisoned her I think—because he wanted his inheritance. She got it all when her husband died of course, and he felt like he'd been cheated."

"Oh, I read that one too," Anna said. "But in that case, the stepmother was a young woman who would have lived for many, many years and spent all of the money his father had left her."

"And remember," Edie said, "Nathan doesn't get it all. He'll have to share his inheritance with his sister."

All eyes turned toward Stephanie.

Maggie had seen her moving among the mourners, her son Kenny in tow. She was a personable young woman and although Maggie doubted that she knew many of the guests, she was mingling successfully.

"Seems altogether too happy to me," Edie commented.

"She's just a generally cheerful person," Victoria said.

"She shouldn't have brought her little boy though." Anna's head moved back and forth in a sad little gesture. "He's too young for a funeral."

"I don't agree," Edie stated. Her voice rang with conviction. "It's good for children to see all sides of life. And she probably didn't have anyone to leave him with. She might have grown up here, but she's been away for a long time."

"You'd think Andrea's nanny could have watched him," Clare said. "She's got to watch the twins after all, and one more wouldn't be such a burden."

"Or with whoever is watching Nathan's daughter," Anna added. "They don't have her along, and little Kenny seems to like his cousin very well."

They all remembered his hopeful query about Caitlin on Saturday morning.

Clare, though, was back in her book about the stepchild who killed his father's bothersome wife and heir. "Just because Nathan has to share his inheritance, it doesn't mean that he didn't do it. They might even have done it together," she added.

The others all stared.

"Do it?" Maggie repeated. "We still don't know exactly how Candy died." Her eyes settled on Louise.

"I like Stephanie," Anna ventured. "We talked some on Saturday, when I helped her get the iced tea. Her husband left her, you know. Just walked out on her and that sweet little boy, for a woman he worked with that was barely out of her teens. They were fairly well-off, but she let him keep everything in the divorce so that he wouldn't fight her for custody."

Victoria raised a brow. "Surely a wife that young wouldn't want to be burdened with a child."

"Probably just send him off to military boarding school," Edie said.

The others stared at her.

"Don't look at me like that. That's what rich people do." Edie nodded, a confirmation of her own statement. "He probably threatened to fight for custody hoping she would do just that."

Maggie had to agree with Edie on that. She'd heard of other similar cases from parents whose children were going through bitter divorces. Some of them never got to see their grandchildren again.

More might have been said on this topic except that Andrea had left her husband talking to a group of choir members and was walking straight toward them.

"Is Alan all right?" Maggie asked, once Andrea had stopped beside them.

Andrea's eyes strayed toward her husband, standing where she'd left him. She gave a short nod. "He's fine. He wants to leave for the office, but I told him it's only natural to take the whole day off."

If there was a polite response to this, Maggie didn't know what it was. So she nodded toward the frail looking young woman sitting beside Nathan. "Is that your brother Nathan's wife?"

"Stepbrother." Andrea automatically corrected her. "And, yes, it is. Dawn."

"Is she well?" Louise frowned. "She seems very pale."

"Perhaps she was very close to your mother?" Anna suggested.

Andrea seemed startled by this. "Oh, no. Mother wasn't close to either Nathan or Stephanie or their families. She didn't consider them relations at all, actually, since there was no blood connection." Andrea glanced around the group of older women as she said this. "It sounds terrible, I know, but Mother was just like that. She could never understand people who adopted children either. She always said that she just couldn't understand how a woman could feel motherly about someone else's child."

Anna looked startled. "But she was making a quilt for Nathan's new baby."

Andrea shrugged. "She did the polite things, the things people expected of a grandmother."

Andrea glanced over at her stepbrother's wife. "Dawn always looks like that. It's that white-blonde hair. It's natural, of course, and she has that white skin to go with it. Makes her look pale all the time. And black is definitely not her color."

Anna agreed that she would probably look well in pastels.

Andrea frowned as she continued to stare at Dawn. "Though she does look even paler than usual." As though just processing Anna's earlier remark, Andrea looked back to her. "Did you say she's pregnant again?" She shook her head slowly and her voice turned cold. "Honestly, Nathan is going to kill that woman. She's had two miscarriages since Caitlin was born. She shouldn't be having babies at all. She's diabetic, you know, and her first pregnancy was difficult."

Andrea moved away abruptly, not even bothering to take her leave.

Edie harrumphed, but the others were more willing to forgive her lack of manners.

"The poor dear just lost her mother," Anna reminded Edie.

Clare was staring at Dawn. "She's diabetic," Clare repeated. "Hmmm . . ."

"Oh, oh. Another book you read?" Maggie had to smile.

But Clare was very serious. "Actually, yes, but a true crime story. And this could be important. Did you know you can kill someone with an overdose of insulin?"

The others stared, but they all recalled a famous court case some years past where an insulin overdose played a large part.

"Humph." Edie straightened her shoulders and headed toward the house. "I'm going to go get some more of that punch. This whole thing is leaving a very bad taste in my mouth."

26

Maggie opened the window to allow the hot air to exit the car. On the driver's side, Bobby did the same. He adjusted the air vents before easing from his spot at the side of the road. As soon as they were under way, he spoke.

"Andrea seems to be taking it well."

"Hmmm." Maggie considered Bobby's words. "Sometimes. But at other times her behavior has been . . ." Maggie hesitated, uncertain how to describe Andrea's recent manner. ". . . Strange," she finally said.

Bobby frowned. "Strange how?"

"It's hard to explain. Sometimes it seems that she's trying too hard to be stoic. But when she spoke to us all at the church on Friday, we thought her attitude was almost insulting. Like she couldn't be bothered with all this on top of her job. As though Candy died just to inconvenience her." Maggie tried to remember her words. "She said it was an especially busy time of year for her at work."

Bobby was shaking his head, but it wasn't at the traffic. Cars were moving smoothly along the 101 loop. "No, Ma, I think you've got her wrong. Andrea's shy and emotional. But she doesn't like to have people see her emotional side. She was like that in school too. Some of the kids thought she was stuck up, but she would just show a calm face to everyone until she could be alone and fall apart. I found her in the parking lot one day, huddled on the seat of her car, crying her eyes out. She'd overheard some of the girls calling her a cold bitch. But the truth was she just didn't know how to interact with other girls. She got on better with the guys."

Bobby stopped speaking for a moment while he changed lanes for their exit.

"I think you were closer to the truth when you said she's trying to be stoic."

Maggie thought over this new insight into Andrea's character.

"How do you think her marriage is?"

Bobby frowned. "I think it's strained."

"What was that business with Alan? Was that part of it?"

"I think he was drunk. But I don't know why he wanted to get drunk at his mother-in-law's funeral. I don't really know him. Maybe he and Nathan just never get along."

"Is that who he was yelling at?"

Bobby nodded as he pulled the car into Maggie's condominium complex.

"What do your old friends think of Alan?"

Bobby stopped the car in front of Maggie's condo, but neither of them moved. The engine idled and cool air continued to stream from the vents.

"Alan isn't real popular with the old high school crowd. He's a bit standoffish. A few of the others think he's jealous of us, since we're mostly men, and think that he tries to keep Andrea from meeting with us. You know, for coffee and conversation, that kind of thing."

"But you don't think that?"

"I don't know, Ma. The truth is, I barely know Andrea any more. We were good friends in high school, but that was a long time ago. I'm working on the assumption that she hasn't changed much. But who knows? It's been a long time."

Yes, Maggie thought. That was the thing all right. Who knows how much a person could change in sixteen years? In high school, Andrea was apparently shy and sweet and insecure. She didn't give that impression today. But no matter how much Maggie wanted to clear Louise of suspicion, she couldn't bring herself to put Andrea in the role of killer. Especially not of her own mother.

27

Michael arrived for his regular Monday night dinner almost an hour late. Maggie had almost given up on him when the doorbell finally rang.

"Sorry, Ma." Michael dropped a kiss on Maggie's cheek and followed her into the kitchen. "Big accident on Hayden and Thomas just at the end of my shift."

"No problem. With Candy's funeral today, I knew I'd be busy. I made stew last night, and I've just had it simmering. It will be better than ever."

Which it was. Within minutes, they were sitting together at the table, Michael tucking into his meal with gusto.

"So how was the funeral?"

"It was real nice, Michael. And the reception was at Andrea's house. You should see it—absolutely beautiful."

Michael was nodding, which caused Maggie to pause.

"You've seen Andrea's house?"

"No. But I know the area. Beautiful homes. Big. Very pricey."

"Hmmm." Maggie was eating, but more slowly than her hungry son. "We were talking about that. How expensive that house must be. Just huge, and beautifully decorated. The pool area looks like a rain forest."

Michael frowned. He stopped eating momentarily so that he could look into his mother's face. "We?"

"Oh, just the other Bee members and I. While we were there, you know."

Michael's frown only deepened. "You aren't getting any ideas about Mrs. Breckner's death now, are you?"

Maggie hoped she looked more innocent than she felt.

"Of course not dear. But what else would we talk about at the funeral other than how she died?"

She had him there and he knew it.

"I don't suppose you heard anything about it down at the police station?"

Michael frowned. Maggie was glad she was his mother. Otherwise that fierce look would have been daunting.

"Ma, I wouldn't tell you if I did. Except to say 'stay out of it'. Come to think of it, I'll say it anyway. Stay out of it, Ma."

"Okay." Maggie pushed at a potato with her fork. She wasn't very hungry but she did want to keep Michael company at the table.

"I'm still worried about Louise though." She put her fork at the side of her plate and looked at Michael. "I was thinking . . . while I waited for you."

"Oh, oh."

Michael said it softly, but Maggie heard him anyway. She ignored him.

"I know you think Candy had a heart attack or something." Maggie put her hand on the table and leaned toward Michael. Her eyes were so intense; he stopped his fork halfway to his mouth. "But if someone did kill her, Michael, then maybe her accident wasn't an accident after all."

Michael's fork returned to his plate as he frowned at his mother. "I see where you're going here, but . . ."

Maggie interrupted before he could go any further with

his rebuttal. "It was a one car accident, Michael. The first accident she ever had, in her whole life. Don't you think someone could have tampered with the brakes or something?"

Michael released a long breath. "Ma, I'm sure her insurance company is checking out the car. I saw the car . . ." His frown turned into a grin. "Why did she drive a sports car anyway? It seemed like such an unlikely car for someone like Mrs. Breckner."

Maggie grinned back as Michael resumed his meal. "An old lady, you mean?"

"Oh, no. I'm not going there again." He laughed. "It's the kind of car a lot of men buy when they have a mid-life crisis. Do women have those?"

Maggie thought about it. "I guess some do. Candy bought that car about two years ago. She fell in love with one Nathan got and determined to have her own. In fact, I think Alan got one too. I remember her laughing about all the business they were giving to Porsche, and how they should get a discount."

Maggie shook her head as memories flooded her mind. "Candy just loved that car. Said it would keep her young. So I guess that might qualify as a sort of mid-life crisis."

Maggie carried her nearly empty plate to the sink. She wasn't going to eat any more; it was silly to pretend she was.

"Women go through a lot of changes in their fifties and sixties. Physical ones, of course, but not only that. Their home lives change because the children are gone. Or they lose their husbands." A wry smile tipped her lips. "Sometimes the kids come home, with kids of their own. I hear a lot about that at the Senior Guild."

Michael shrugged. "I don't think you have to worry

about that, Ma. Not enough room in here for a whole family."

"You're trying to change the subject, Michael." Maggie frowned at her son. "I'm trying to find a way to clear Louise, and don't you see? If someone tried to kill Candy before—by tampering with her car—then Louise would be cleared. No one could imagine her doing something like that. They seem to be concentrating on the fight she and Candy had last week, and the fact that she was there to perform CPR. An earlier murder attempt would have to clear her."

Michael finished his meal and pushed the plate away. He reached for his mother's hand, and covered it with his own. "Ma, I know what you're trying to do. I'm just telling you that getting involved in attempted murder is dangerous. Whatever happened, just let the police handle it, okay?"

With a deep sigh, Maggie agreed. But she kept her eyes lowered as she did. She didn't want Michael to see the rebellious look she was certain was there. Because she was determined to help her friend. There was nothing dangerous about asking questions and making logical deductions. And that's all she and the Bee women planned to do.

28

"Nice turnout."

"Such beautiful music."

Maggie listened to Clare, Anna and the others as they repeated many of the same comments and compliments about Candy's funeral that were made the previous day at the post service reception. There was also a lengthy discussion of Andrea's beautiful house and yard, especially the "rain forest" landscaping around the pool.

Finally, the discussion moved from material things to people.

"I must admit I was surprised to learn of Candy's attitude toward her stepchildren," Victoria commented. "She always struck me as a very modern woman, but that whole thing about there being no blood connection is archaic."

"None of them seem especially broken up over their loss." Edie dismissed the whole family with a single click of her tongue. "Andrea is a cold fish, if you ask me. And her husband is uncouth. Imagine shouting that way during his mother-in-law's funeral reception!"

Clare appeared more somber than usual. "Nathan and Stephanie did the right thing, though. They were there, and properly dressed in black too."

"I don't think Stephanie should have included her little boy, though," Anna said. "Six is too young for funerals."

A debate ensued over whether or not children should attend funerals, and the proper age for them to start. It was several minutes before the conversation returned to the previous day's reception.

"Wasn't it Nathan that Alan was yelling at?" Maggie asked. "I couldn't be certain, since I didn't look up until he started shouting. But Nathan was there beside him, and he seemed to be trying to placate him about something."

The others were as uncertain as Maggie. Until Louise spoke up.

"Vince heard what happened."

All eyes turned from the quilt top to Louise.

"Vince was on the patio with some of the other men from the Senior Guild. Alan was there, offering the men something stronger to drink. Vince said most of them declined as it was so early in the afternoon and they could see that Alan had already had too much. Then Nathan strolled over and greeted the Guild men with a smile. Vince said Alan just rounded on him and started yelling. 'What are you so happy about? Glad you're finally getting all that money, aren't you? You'll make a bundle from her death.' Stuff like that. Vince said it was very embarrassing."

"What did Nathan do?" Clare was brightly alert now, aware that this might support her theory about the stepson killing the stepmother.

"Vince said he conducted himself very well. With dignity, I think he said. Spoke calmly and tried to get Alan to go inside for some coffee. That's when Alan really raised his voice and told him that he didn't need any coffee and what was he trying to imply." Louise had lowered her head and taken a few stitches as she spoke. Now she looked up again. "That's when we all heard him, and when Andrea went over. She got him into the house without a problem and no one saw him again until they came back outside together and he apologized."

"They weren't gone too long," Maggie observed. "I suppose she poured coffee into him."

"They had a few words, too, according to one of Vince's friends," Louise said. "Sam Previnski was in the house using the restroom when they went inside. When he rejoined the others, he claimed he had heard them in the bedroom, arguing."

"What about?"

Clare asked the question, but Maggie was almost as anxious to hear the answer. There was something going on there. Probably, just marital problems. So many marriages didn't last these days. But with their suspicions about Candy's death, and the police seemingly focused on Louise, anything that seemed irregular was worth looking into.

Louise, however, didn't have any more information. Sam had just heard raised voices and hadn't tried to eavesdrop. "Vince said he was embarrassed as it was, just from hearing the sound of an argument. He's a shy sort of man, very quiet, especially around women. I don't think he ever married. I suppose that made him more embarrassed, hearing a married couple arguing in the bedroom."

Anna nodded solemnly. Being the shy sort herself, Maggie felt sure Anna identified with Sam.

"Did you see Nathan's wife?" Anna asked. "Such a somber little thing and white as a sheet. Andrea said she's had two miscarriages since their little girl was born." Anna's sympathy for the woman was evident.

"She might be worried about their financial situation too," Clare said. "Nathan's company isn't doing well. And her pregnant again, too."

Maggie looked up. "Hal mentioned the same thing at

brunch the other day. About Nathan's company. How did you hear about it, Clare?"

"I saw it in the paper," Clare replied. "I've been reading the financial section," she added with a sigh. "Gerald has been trying to teach me about finances and economics. He insists on it, though it's not something I enjoy. He says that most women outlive their husbands, so it's important for me to understand these things."

Maggie and Anna, both widows, agreed with Gerald.

"It is important," Anna said. "I was lost when Jerome died. He always handled all our financial affairs and told me not to worry my pretty head about them. I had to learn fast, and it was hard. I made some expensive mistakes. I was lucky that Carol asked me to come out and live with her. Bill is very good about advising me on financial matters. He doesn't just tell me what to do, he makes sure I know why I'm doing it."

"You say there was a mention of Nathan's company not doing well in the newspaper?" Victoria's voice showed her surprise.

"Oh, yes. Actually, it was an article about speculators who bought up land for development without taking into account the new attitude in the valley toward conservation."

Maggie's eyes widened as she looked at Clare. This was certainly different from her usual "I read something like that in a mystery book."

"Apparently Nathan bought up a large tract of land in North Scottsdale," Clare continued. "Or rather, his development company did. But he hasn't been able to get his plan for the development approved. He wants a higher density for the houses than the zoning allows."

"It used to be easy to get that kind of change approved,"

Maggie said, as she pulled her new thread through the fabric, burying the knot in the batting. "But lately the surrounding homeowners are getting much more active about keeping their areas the way they were meant to be in the city's plan. The environmentalists support the lesser density in the projects too, and with both groups, they can pack the zoning meetings."

"It must be frustrating for him, not being able to get on with his project," Clare said. "This was going to be the biggest thing he'd ever attempted."

"I hate to say this," Victoria began. "But the fact that his business needs money, and that his stepmother just died and left him an inheritance could be important."

Maggie agreed. "I thought the same thing when I heard about it on Sunday," she said. "I meant to tell you all about it, but forgot. The funeral and everything else just drove it from my mind."

Maggie traveled her needle to the next spot she wanted to stitch, and then spoke again. "When I was talking to Michael last night, I had an idea I want to fly by all of you." Maggie concentrated on putting her needle in and out; she was afraid her idea was silly. "It occurred to me that if someone has killed Candy, then maybe her accident wasn't so accidental after all."

Maggie almost held her breath, but it was unnecessary. The reaction to her words was immediate and overwhelmingly favorable.

"We should have thought of this long ago," Clare lamented.

"Oh, my." Anna's response was quieter, but she was no less upset.

"Is there any way we can find out the real cause of the accident?" Clare asked.

"I don't know," Maggie admitted. "Michael thought I was crazy, of course, but he did say the insurance people will probably check it out."

"It would mean that someone other than an Angel of Death killed her," Victoria pointed out.

There was silent stitching for a time as they all thought about this. If the accident had been a murder attempt, then it was probably someone in Candy's family who wanted her dead.

"There's something else I almost forgot," Maggie said. "It came up at brunch on Sunday." Maggie stopped sewing and looked over at Louise. "Something I find worrying. And that you need to hear, Louise."

Louise looked up; she had been concentrating on her stitching. Although she insisted there was nothing to worry about, Maggie was sure Louise was concerned about Candy's death and the questions the police were asking. Louise had been much too quiet, and there were dark circles under her eyes. Maggie suspected she wasn't sleeping well.

Louise smiled at Maggie. "I wish you'd stop worrying about me, Maggie. I keep telling you, the police questions are just routine. Vince agrees. We found her body, and I did what I've been trained to do. There's nothing to worry about."

"But that's just it." Maggie put down her needle. This was important and she wanted to devote her whole attention to it. "Sara told me that she saw a follow-up to that television show about the Angel of Death. It was about a nurse in Ohio who had been arrested—and I think was on trial—for the murder of several patients. Only in this case, instead of trying to ease terminally ill patients' sufferings, she was creating emergencies so that she could act the hero by saving them."

"Ohhh."

Anna's long exhalation, quiet though it was, echoed through the silent room. Maggie knew it reflected the thoughts of all the women around the quilt frame. It was obvious from their expressions that they immediately saw the implication. And this was no mystery novel emulating their circumstances. This was an actual case, something that had really happened.

"Did Detective Warner ask if you'd ever seen Louise save someone's life by administering CPR?" Maggie asked. Maggie's eyes moved around the frame, stopping briefly on the face of each of the Bee members.

There were nods all around. Louise, Maggie noted, was very pale.

"*Now* do you believe me when I say we have to figure out what happened here?" Maggie asked. "Before they come and arrest you!"

29

"I was the last one here to see Candy alive, you know."

The Quilting Bee members were moving about in the bright day room at the Palo Verde Care Center, helping the patients work on individual projects. They had arrived shortly after lunch, laden down with supplies from Candy's sewing room. What better way to use some of her things than with these former friends of hers?

Maggie's only regret was that Louise had declined to join them at the care center. She claimed a prior engagement with Vince, but Maggie was convinced she wanted to stay away from the care center because of the ongoing investigation into Candy's death.

The demonstration of rotary cutting and hand piecing had gone well. To their delight, a dozen patients expressed interest in learning about quilting—ten women, and two men. Now, with the demonstration over, all twelve were working diligently at hand piecing a nine-patch block.

The woman who spoke into a quiet moment caught everyone's attention, visitors and residents alike. All over the room, needles stilled and heads popped up. Maggie, already standing near the table where the woman sat, took two steps to bring her up beside her. She didn't want to miss anything she said.

The speaker was small and stooped, her weathered face

so wrinkled and shriveled it resembled nothing so much as that of a dried apple doll. Her hands were covered with age spots, her fingers bent with arthritis. She'd told Maggie that she was recovering from surgery after breaking her hip.

"She was very excited, she was. Had these bright colored quilt blocks all made up, and was showing them off to me. She told me she would show me how to sew them too if I wanted. And I did want." She took another stitch, pushing her needle through the fabric and pulling it out the length of her thread. "This here sewing is good exercise for the arthritis, you know. You have to keep using your fingers or they don't want to move at all."

Several other women nodded their agreement.

"Well, I'm glad we were able to come over and help you with this," Maggie said. "I guess Candy wasn't able to give you a lesson after all."

"Oh, she started," the woman went on.

Maggie bit at her lower lip. What *was* the woman's name? Her memory just seemed to get worse and worse. Then, without warning, the name leapt into her consciousness. Carolina. She remembered commenting on what a pretty name it was when she first heard it, much to the bearer's delight.

Carolina set her stitching down on the tabletop, and smiled demurely at the attention she had garnered. Not only the Bee women, but most of the other patients as well, had stopped what they were doing to look at her as she spoke.

"She was so enthusiastic, she started right in with the lesson. She took a couple of fabric squares and she showed me how to line them up and pin them and all. But then her children came to visit and I had to leave. Candy said I could stay, but I could tell the kids didn't want me there." She smiled again. "But she gave me the two squares she pinned, with two others, and the needle and thread and all, so I could practice. I've got it right here." She reached into her pocket, drawing out a wrinkled four-patch square of yellow and olive green.

Maggie reached for the quilt block, murmuring compliments on the work. But at the same time, she looked toward Victoria, her eyebrows raised in silent inquiry. Kids? Maggie mouthed. Victoria nodded. She too had caught the plural. And they weren't the only ones.

"Was it her daughter Andrea and her husband?" Clare asked.

From the eagerness in her voice, Maggie knew Clare hoped this would be a good clue. These visitors may have been the last to see Candy alive—could even have some knowledge of how she died. Might even have helped her die, though the Angel of Death theory seemed more and more remote.

Carolina's voice was every bit as enthusiastic as Clare's.

"Oh, no, it was the brother and sister."

Maggie could just hear Carolina thinking, *Nothing like a good gossip*. The relish of being the first to share this news was in her voice, and there was a sparkle in her eyes. She settled her hands comfortably on the table in front of her, the needle still clutched in her crooked fingers.

"I know Candy just had the one daughter. But she had those two from her husband's side. They smiled nice and all when they came to visit, but I could tell Candy wasn't as happy to see them as she was when her daughter came."

"We met them both," Victoria said. "They seem like nice young people."

"Candy was making that four-patch quilt for Nathan's new baby," Anna told Carolina.

"Yeah, she told me. She didn't seem too happy about it neither. Said something about the mother's health."

"She's a diabetic," Clare told her.

"So am I," said the quiet woman sitting beside Carolina. Searching her memory for a name Maggie was delighted to find it. Evelyn. Almost as wide as she was tall, Maggie wondered if Evelyn was in the care center to get her weight under control. Her wide girth couldn't be good for her heart, and if she was diabetic she might have other problems as well.

"It's not so bad, except for having to poke your finger all the time," Evelyn said. "And my feet are always cold. But it would be hard to get through a pregnancy without complications. Dangerous for the baby too."

Maggie decided she'd heard enough of ailments. Reaching across the table, she picked up the gentleman's block—his name was Fred Smith, but he'd urged them to call him Smitty—and held it up. "Smitty has finished sewing his first two rows together. Let me show you how to fit them together so that the seams meet properly."

With that, the Bee women scattered, finding stitchers who had finished their rows, and demonstrating how to line up and pin the pieces. While Maggie showed Smitty how to move the seam fabric from one side to the other so that he could sew through it rather than over it, Carolina returned to the subject of Candy.

"Don't you think it was odd how she was so scared to stay here, and then she died? And the police are asking questions too."

Maggie held out a pin for Smitty but didn't comment.

"She told me that she told her kids and her friends about how scared she was. She didn't think she'd leave here alive, unless she went right away." Carolina had begun speaking with relish, enjoying imparting some new gossip. But now her voice changed, obviously sympathizing with Candy. "But no one would take her out of here."

Maggie sympathized with Candy too, but there were more practical considerations.

"Well, she did have two broken legs," Maggie said. "It would have been difficult for anyone to take care of her unless they knew just how to do so. Here she had the professional help she needed."

Smitty took the proffered pin and Maggie held out another.

"Well, I guess." Carolina agreed, but grudgingly. "I wasn't so sure about that Angel of Death thing myself, but I do think it's mighty peculiar that Candy died like that. She sure wasn't acting sick or anything."

Maggie's eyes remained on Smitty's block as he pinned, but her mind was busy contemplating Carolina's comments. It certainly agreed with common opinion within the Bee. Candy had been much better when they saw her on Wednesday.

"You know, she thought Joseph here might be one of them there Angels of Death like she heard about on the television show."

Carolina surprised Maggie by giving Joseph a smile that was purely flirtatious. On her wrinkled face, the girlish gesture was so incongruous; Maggie had to bite her cheek to control a smile.

"But we all know Joseph would never do anything so wicked."

Joseph, who was helping them with the group, blushed even as he returned Carolina's flirty smile with one of his own. Maggie hadn't wanted to like the young man. As a stranger, he made such a good suspect—so much better than anyone in Candy's family, all of whom were personal acquaintances. And there was something particularly terrible about a child killing a parent, even a stepparent.

But Maggie found that she did like Joseph. He was a personable young man and seemed to genuinely enjoy interacting with the elderly patients. Best of all, he had a gift for making them laugh. And wasn't laughter one of the best medicines around?

Maggie had to bite her cheek to keep from laughing herself as Carolina actually winked at Joseph.

"You would never kill anyone, would you, Joey honey?"

30

"Joey honey" flashed Carolina a wide smile. It was obvious why the man was so popular with the patients. Charm oozed from him. The flirty smile, the fun sparkling in his dark eyes. Yet Candy had supposedly disliked him. Why did she accuse him? Surely there were many other employees—wouldn't it have served her better to choose someone less popular than Joseph?

"Miss Carolina, hon," Joseph said. "You know I could never do anything to hurt any of you sweet folks here. You're like my family."

Carolina, and even the more serious Evelyn, giggled. So did several of the other women. But even more surprising to Maggie, the men smiled too.

"Joseph is one of the Palo Verde's assets," Smitty told them. "He keeps us cheered up, and helps those who can't get around on their own. Don't know what I'd do without Joseph," he finished with a nod.

Maggie glanced at Smitty, noting the sincerity of his statement and remembering that he had entered the room slowly using a walker. She recalled seeing Joseph beside him.

Joseph smiled. "Yeah, Smitty likes to go into the garden in the afternoons. I usually help him find a nice bench or table to sit at. You ladies have sidetracked him today."

"I'm enjoying this," Smitty said. "My wife used to quilt. I'm sorry I never tried it when she was still with me. It would have been nice working on a quilt together."

Maggie watched him blink rapidly a few times. Reaching for his block, she examined it carefully while he swallowed. When he was back in control of his emotions, she held up the block for all to see.

"Smitty is fast, ladies. He's all done with his block already. And his work is very good too. Look at how nicely all four seams come together." Maggie pointed to each of the corners of the center square, where four of the fabric squares met. "That's very difficult for a beginner," Maggie added; she didn't want the others to feel inadequate if their own work was not so perfect.

The others at his table leaned forward to see. The block passed from hand to hand with suitable congratulatory exclamations.

"I was an engineer," Smitty told them proudly.

"No wonder you did such nice even stitches."

Maggie could see that Victoria's complement pleased him.

"I'm ready to try another one," Smitty announced with a grin, thoughts of his beloved wife once again consigned to memory. "Pass those fabric squares this way."

The basket of fabric was sent down the table and Smitty began to sort through it, looking for another nine pieces to stitch together.

While the other Bee members continued to supervise their students, Maggie moved closer to Joseph.

"So you knew about the allegations Candy made against you." She kept her voice low.

Joseph nodded. The engaging grin was gone. "She didn't like me. I never knew why, though. I treated her like I do all the patients here. I flatter them a little and joke with them. Most of them enjoy it."

Maggie frowned. "Did she think you were patronizing her?"

Joseph frowned. "I don't know. Maybe she just didn't like my jokes, or the way I look. Who knows? But when the police asked all those questions after she died, I knew it was because of that." His frown deepened, and the look in his eyes was no longer friendly. "She caused me a lot of trouble, not only with the police but with the care center people. I'm lucky I didn't lose my job."

Maggie put her hand on his arm. "I've seen you with the patients, Joseph. I know you do an excellent job. And you work days, don't you? Candy particularly mentioned that the suspicious deaths had been at night. In fact . . ."

Maggie was ready to tell him about the other accusations Candy had made against staff members, when Tara suddenly appeared.

"How's it going in here?" she asked.

She flashed a brilliant smile around the room, though Maggie thought her eyes lingered a little too long on the two of them, standing to one side with their heads together. Tara used a bright, chirpy voice, the kind that Maggie usually associated with pre-school and kindergarten teachers. But at least she hadn't used that awful royal we nurses sometimes affected.

"Everything is going very well," Victoria replied. "Smitty was the first to finish his block."

"And Evelyn and Joann have finished as well," Clare added.

Voices called out from various parts of the room, and hands held up finished blocks for Tara to admire.

Carolina, still stitching, frowned. "I'm getting there. I

been talking with the quilting ladies. It's nice to have some new people to visit with."

Tara laughed. "I know you, Carolina. You mean you've been gossiping. I hope you aren't telling tales about the other patients."

Maggie's eyebrows raised in surprise as she met Victoria's eyes across the room. She was surprised to hear Tara voice her fears so openly. And she thought she was being paranoid when she had the fleeting notion that the head nurse had wanted to interrupt her private conversation with Joseph. Now she found herself wondering.

"We been talking about Candy. She started teaching me to sew these here quilt blocks, you know."

Maggie thought Tara's smile lost some of its sparkle, but before the head nurse could comment, Carolina cut her thread and held up her block.

"Look at that. I finished, and it looks pretty darn good, too."

Everyone laughed at Carolina's confidence, admiring her block and agreeing that it was indeed "good."

Maggie approached the table, leaving Joseph to get back to whatever duties might await him. She stopped next to Tara, who was admiring the stitchers' blocks.

"Joseph was just telling us that Smitty usually spends his afternoons in the garden. I've been admiring that garden ever since I first saw it, and wondered if it would be all right to go out for a closer look."

Maggie glanced around the table at their students, who were all engrossed in their work. Everyone had finished or almost finished one block. They were stitching more confidently now as they proceeded to start a second.

Tara nodded, even gracing Maggie with a smile. "Sure. You can go outside. It is a beautiful garden. But you will have to take one of the staff with you. We monitor all guests for security purposes."

Maggie must have appeared as startled as she felt, for Tara was quick with an explanation.

"It's not what you might be thinking. It's just that we have a lot of Alzheimer's patients. Many of them like to work in the garden, so we let them. But we have to be careful that no one wanders off. They get lost so easily." Her eyes darted around the room. Joseph was still there, squatting next to a tiny woman in a wheelchair who was seated near the television. Tara nodded in his direction. "Joseph will take you. Just tell him I said it was okay."

31

Maggie welcomed the dry heat of the garden after the artificial coolness of the air-conditioned interior. The quality of light seemed better too, the harsh fluorescent glare replaced by clear sunlight filtered through the leaves of tall trees. The pleasant scent of freshly cut grass led her to draw in a deep breath.

"Mmm . . ." Maggie smiled at Joseph beside her. "This is nice. I can see why Smitty likes it out here."

Joseph nodded. "This is my favorite spot in the whole place, and there are some nice spots."

Maggie recalled her first sight of him asleep on the staff lounge sofa and wondered if that was another of his "nice spots."

Joseph directed Maggie toward a long stone bench, shaded by a feathery acacia and backed by a blooming oleander hedge.

"Smitty can sew out here tomorrow afternoon," Maggie suggested.

Joseph replied with a shrug. "If he wants to keep doing it."

It was Maggie's turn to nod. She'd spotted her prey at the opposite side of the garden. The arranged accident idea was firmly lodged in her brain now, which made the Angel of Death thing even more unlikely. But she still wanted to meet the various people Candy had accused. She was plotting how she could ditch Joseph and approach the gardener when the matter was settled for her.

A woman kneeling beside a flowerbed adjacent to their bench saw Joseph and waved her hand at him. Maggie had noticed her, because she had the sweetest face she'd ever seen. Her skin was smooth and young looking, belying the brown hair liberally sprinkled with gray that surrounded her round face. But her pale brown eyes showed no sparkle, no interest in things around her. And her gesture reminded Maggie of elementary school, when just such hand waving alerted the teacher that one wished to visit the girls' room.

And it seemed that was exactly what this woman wanted to do. Joseph excused himself to Maggie, promised he wouldn't be long, and proceeded into the care center with his new companion. She had placed her hand in Joseph's, and walked complacently alongside him.

Perfect, Maggie thought. As soon as the two were inside, Maggie scuttled off the bench and hurried across the lawn. Almost exactly opposite her, a man in jeans and a polo shirt was hunched over, mulching a flowerbed. Small in stature and dark skinned, he was everyone's preconception of a Southwestern gardener. Though Maggie did think the polo shirt an incongruous touch. Most gardeners wore plain T-shirts, some long-sleeved shirts to protect their arms. A polo shirt seemed very suburban.

"Hello," Maggie called as she approached the flowerbed where he worked. She used her friendliest voice and hoped he spoke English. Her Spanish was not up to the conversation she wanted to have.

The man who rose and turned to meet her was older than she expected—perhaps as much as forty. And when he spoke, she found his English much better than anticipated.

In fact, it was the speech of a well-educated man.

"Hello," he replied. "Were you speaking to me?"

"Yes." Maggie hoped she managed to contain her astonishment at his excellent English. Just in case, she pulled out her best smile. "I've been admiring your handiwork. The gardens here are just lovely."

"Thank you. I enjoy working with plants."

"You do an excellent job." Maggie swallowed. She might just as well plunge right in. One of the advantages of gray hair was that no one was surprised if you acted nosy. And it was a much quicker way of obtaining answers than trying to finesse them from another.

Self-consciously, she ran her fingers through her short hair.

"Excuse my impertinence . . ." She smiled again, hoping that would help smooth her way. "Your English is excellent. You seem quite well educated." Maggie hesitated.

"For a gardener?"

He smiled. Thin lines around his mouth appeared and deepened. Beneath the brim of his baseball cap, Maggie could see that humor beamed from his shaded eyes.

Maggie, feeling more comfortable, returned the smile. "Well, yes." She offered her hand. "Maggie Browne."

The man opposite her held back a moment, as though uncertain whether he should take her hand. Then, apparently making a decision, he removed his glove, wiped his hand on his jeans and offered it. "Antonio Suarez."

He nodded his head in a slight bow. It was a gentlemanly, old-world gesture. Maggie couldn't have been more charmed if he'd kissed the back of her hand.

"Mr. Suarez." Maggie nodded in her turn. "I'm happy to meet you."

"Please. Call me Antonio."

Maggie smiled. "And it's Maggie." She glanced around

her. "I don't know when I've seen such a lovely garden. Do you have a degree in landscaping?"

"No. I merely enjoy working with the plants. Giving plants life and helping them grow is all I can do for now."

His eyes showed a yearning so deep it startled Maggie. But not nearly as much as his next statement.

"Actually, I am a doctor."

Maggie's eyes widened. "A doctor?"

"Yes. A medical doctor. At least I was in El Salvador. But I had to leave."

He sighed, and Maggie understood that he had not left willingly.

"My brothers became involved in politics. They chose the wrong side, however." He offered Maggie a wry smile. "I was busy in my clinic, and was not interested in politics. But I became involved anyway because my brothers and uncles were. The men in power would not have believed that I do not care about such things. When my brothers fled, I had to leave too."

"And you aren't able to practice here?"

Antonio shook his head. "Not yet. It is a difficult process. I am going through the steps, but they are many and complicated. The Dillions have been very kind in sponsoring me. They allow my family to live here on the property and I work in the garden."

He gestured toward a small house at the rear corner of the garden. Maggie had not even noticed it behind the banks of blooming bougainvillea that covered the walls.

"Oh, yes. I just recently learned that the Dillions own the care home. Tara went to school with my son. I hadn't seen her since their high school days, until I was here visiting a friend and she recognized me."

"Your friend, I hope she is all right."

"I'm afraid she passed away. Rather suddenly," Maggie added, watching carefully for his reaction. There was none that she could see, except for sympathy at her loss.

"Before she died, my friend told us a strange story about an Angel of Death," Maggie began. She went on to explain to him about the television program and Candy's paranoia. She had just finished the tale when Joseph reappeared.

"Are you ready to go back inside, Maggie? Looks like the quilters are all going great guns in there." He smiled at her, nodding a greeting toward Antonio.

"I wonder if I could have another minute with Antonio?" Maggie asked.

Joseph raised one brow, but didn't otherwise comment. He drifted toward a bench where he joined an elderly man leafing through a magazine.

"Yes, the police have asked me about this matter," Antonio told Maggie. "You say she thought I was the one?"

Maggie watched Antonio carefully. She thought the bewildered look on his face was real.

"She named three different people. It seems that each time she told someone who she suspected, she named a different person."

"A troubled woman," Antonio murmured, shaking his head. He frowned. "I told the police when they asked. That day, I was here with the patients, just as I am every day. The evenings, I spend with my wife and son."

Maggie nodded. Of course he would have an alibi. These things were never easy.

"Thank you for speaking with me. I hope you aren't angry with me for bringing it up. I truly don't suspect anyone myself. I'm just collecting information, hoping it will lead somewhere. I'm afraid if I don't, the police may arrest my dear friend."

She had told him how Louise tried to revive Candy with CPR.

"You must do what you can to help your friend. I am not angry."

Maggie smiled warmly as he took her hand again. What a kindly gentleman he was. No matter how anxious she was to find a suspect—and a suspect that was not a close friend—she just could not see this sadly treated individual as a cold-hearted killer.

"It's been a real pleasure meeting you, Antonio. I wish you good luck here in this country."

Maggie shook his hand again. Then she set off to alert Joseph that she was ready to return inside.

32

A car full of eager listeners settled themselves for the ride back to the church. Without Louise's van, Clare had driven her roomy Cadillac, which made for easier conversation; the seats were closer together, and the interior was very quiet.

Clare was eager to hear all about the gardener. So were the others. Maggie, however, was aware of only the olive tree as the car passed beneath it. She found herself peering into its thick branches, and felt a shiver shimmy up her spine.

Victoria seemed to sense what Maggie was feeling. "I don't see any owls today."

Her quiet voice made Maggie feel silly, and she made an effort to smile about their earlier experience—and her obvious fears.

Edie, however, was determined to see a dire warning in the supposed omen.

"Didn't I tell you?" Edie reminded them. "About the sky that first day? This place looks pretty, but there's evil here." She pressed her head forward then back in a decisive nod.

"Evil?" Anna repeated.

Maggie let out her breath with a loud whoosh.

"Edie, listen to yourself. You're getting as paranoid as Candy." Her voice was gently chiding. "There's no evil there. That sounds like an ad for a horror movie."

Edie pulled her lips into a severe line and refrained from answering. But everyone could see she stood by her statement.

Maggie sighed.

"Never mind that," Clare said from her position in the driver's seat. "Tell us about the gardener. I saw you talking to him."

"A very interesting man," Maggie began. "Very nice, obviously intelligent. His English is excellent. And he has lovely manners, kind of European."

Maggie went on to recount as much of their conversation as she could remember. The others listened in fascinated silence.

"A doctor?" Anna said. "Imagine that."

"That means he would know about all kinds of things that could help him kill people," Clare said. "Ways that wouldn't be noticed, maybe."

"But I thought we decided that someone tried to kill Candy earlier, in the car accident?" Anna was confused. "If that's so, then there isn't an Angel of Death after all, is there?"

"Well, you never know," Edie said.

"We always thought that story unlikely," Maggie countered. "But we should check out all the theories. Just in case."

"We don't know that Candy's accident wasn't just a question of her losing control of her car, either," Clare reminded Anna. "I do wish we could find out," she added.

Maggie silently agreed.

"Does Antonio seem like a man who would support euthanasia?" Victoria asked, bringing the conversation back to its original subject.

"He didn't strike me that way, but there's no telling, is there?" Maggie usually trusted her instincts about people, but this man came from a world completely outside her experience. She didn't know Antonio at all. But, darn, she had liked the man with his quiet voice and gallant manner. "Personally, I found him very kind and gentlemanly."

"So you believe his story?" Edie asked. "About being a doctor, and seeking political asylum and everything?"

"I don't see any reason not to," Maggie replied. "It would certainly be easy enough to check his story with Tara. Remember, I told him that I knew her."

They had pulled into the church parking lot, but no one was ready to get out of the car.

"There is one interesting thing," Maggie continued. "He and his family live right there on the grounds. There's a small house at the back of the garden. It's very difficult to see because it's covered with bougainvillea."

"That means he *could* have been there at night then."

Clare mentioned what had seemed an insurmountable problem concerning the gardener as suspect. The other obstacle—medical knowledge—had already been addressed.

The five women stared uneasily at one another. The more they delved into Candy's death, the more confusing it became. This new information might mean good news for Louise. But had Maggie spent the afternoon with a murderer?

33

The visit to the Palo Verde Care Center remained the topic of choice the following morning. It was warm on Wednesday, even early in the day, and they were stitching in their cool, air-conditioned room. The quilting was moving along, and the frame would be rolled again by the end of the morning. As they stitched, they repeated every detail of the previous day's lesson for Louise. Then Maggie had to recount her talks with Joseph and Antonio.

"I still can't believe the gardener is a doctor," Clare said.

"It's better than one of your novels, isn't it?" Maggie smiled at Clare, sitting opposite her at the frame.

"This would make a good novel," Clare agreed. "But there has to be an ending. You can't have a novel end without the police arresting the bad guy."

"We seem to have cleared all of our suspects," Victoria commented. "At least, all the Angel of Death suspects."

"Oh, dear, we have, haven't we?" Anna said. "We agreed earlier that Tara might want to stop Candy's rumors of an Angel of Death, but killing Candy would just make those rumors worse."

"It would seem to add credence," Victoria said.

"And we all met Joseph yesterday," Clare began, as the others nodded. "I liked him. I can't imagine such a nice young man killing anyone. He genuinely enjoys working with the older people."

Edie almost snorted her usual "humph!" "That's what they always say. Anytime a serial killer or a rapist is arrested, all his friends and neighbors go on television saying how shocked they are because he was such a nice man."

Maggie had to admit that Edie had a point. Still, even if she had to call it woman's intuition, she found it difficult to believe either Tara, Joseph or Antonio was a killer.

"We all did think Candy's theory about an Angel of Death was pretty far-fetched," Maggie reminded them yet again.

"When she was alive," Clare added.

"But if the people she named are all no longer suspects," Anna asked, "who killed Candy?"

"Well, we have to go back to her car accident, and consider if it was set up or not." Maggie's recommendation met with approval. "Who would have access to her car without arousing suspicion."

"In mystery books," Clare said, "the police always suspect the family first."

Maggie, Louise and Edie all nodded their agreement.

"But isn't that usually when there's a husband or a wife?" Anna asked. Her forehead wrinkled. "Or even a boyfriend or girlfriend. Candy was alone."

"But she did have family," Maggie said.

"Mystery books also say to follow the money trail," Victoria added.

"Do you mean Andrea?" Clare frowned. "I don't know. I hate to think she could have been involved in her own mother's death."

"I think she means Nathan," Maggie said. "He and Stephanie will get quite a bit too. Ken was a successful businessman and very well-off when he died, and he left his estate to Candy only for her lifetime."

"Candy told me about her will one day," Anna said. "Andrea doesn't get anything. Candy put everything in a trust fund for her grandchildren. The house and everything from Ken, goes to Nathan and Stephanie of course. But she had a nice income from her first husband for Andrea. It was when Andrea started her business and became so successful that she changed her will. She was telling me about the trust and how to set one up." Anna smiled. "She didn't seem to realize that I don't have the kind of income she did."

"Well, that takes care of another suspect," Clare said.

"Yes, and I'm glad," Victoria replied. "I never liked considering her as a suspect in her own mother's death."

"One of the women we met yesterday claims to be the last one to have seen Candy alive." Clare looked toward Louise as she spoke. "Remember?" Her gaze scanned the others. "She said that when she left Candy, Nathan and Stephanie were there with her."

"That Nathan had a motive," Edie said.

Louise raised her brows at Clare's last bit of intelligence, but didn't speculate on its implication. Instead she just shook her head. "I know what you all are trying to do, and believe me I appreciate it. But I don't want any of you to get into trouble. You can't accuse someone of murder that way, Edie."

But Edie showed no regret. "They might do the same thing to you. And it won't be just some old ladies talking, then, but big men with badges and guns. And handcuffs," she added for good measure.

All the Bee members paled at the thought. Anna caught her breath in with a rasp that had the others asking after her in concern.

Maggie blessed Victoria, not for the first time, for her impeccable sense of timing.

"The patients were very excited about the lottery drawing tonight," she said. Her voice was quiet, as usual, her tone conversational. "It was while you were outside with the gardener, Maggie."

"Oh, yes." Anna picked up on the new conversational thread, relieved at no longer being the center of attention. "One of the nurses was going to purchase tickets for anyone who wanted them. They were having a lot of fun dreaming of what they would buy with the winnings."

"That's right." Clare pushed her needle into the top while she reached for the spool of thread. "Tonight's jackpot is higher than it's been for two years. Almost a hundred million dollars. And they say it will probably reach that before the drawing time tonight." She paused with the cut length of thread in one hand, the needle in the other, a dreamy expression on her face. "Imagine what you could do with that much money."

"We should buy some tickets," Edie declared. "We can pool our money like the office people do."

"Why, Edie. Do you buy lottery tickets?" Maggie's tone was teasing. She would have thought Edie more likely to rant about how people wasted their hard-earned money on worthless tickets.

"I don't usually buy tickets," Edie admitted. "But the jackpot is so high right now. And someone has to win. Why not take a chance? A lot of the big winners are office pools."

Maggie had to smile as she saw pink seep into Edie's cheeks. "I don't buy them either. But I like your idea. Let's do it."

Like teenage girls at a pajama party sharing secrets, the women took turns speaking of what they would do with their shares if they were the lucky recipients of the hundred million.

With dreams still in mind, they put together five dollars apiece. Maggie agreed to stop at the Circle K on the way home and purchase their tickets. "You don't mind stopping, do you, Victoria?"

"Oh, no. It will be a new experience for me."

"Of course, we'd have to give at least ten percent to St. Rose."

Clare's declaration seemed to bring them back to earth. They all agreed that if they won, they would first of all present a check to St. Rose. With this virtuous vow, Maggie and Victoria headed to the nearby Circle K, the others to their homes.

34

"I guess we shouldn't be surprised," Maggie told Victoria, as they stood at the end of a long line at the Circle K. "After all, we don't usually buy tickets, and here we are. I'll bet a lot of these other people are just getting them today because of the big jackpot too."

The woman standing immediately in front of them turned.

"You said it. I always get one here, every week. But this is unreal. Lots of people only come out for the big prizes." Her disgusted gaze moved up the line.

Maggie felt that she was accusing them with her stare. But then, they *were* guilty of clogging the line and making it longer than usual. Neither of them had ever purchased a ticket before today.

In front of her, another woman turned. "It's that guy up there now. He's holding everything up because he's buying two hundred tickets. Can you imagine?"

"Two hundred tickets!" Victoria repeated. "Goodness!"

Maggie looked, wondering what kind of person spent two hundred dollars on lottery tickets. Even though the prize money was high, the odds of winning were so astronomical she could barely justify the five dollars she was contributing to the Bee's pot. But it was one thing to throw in a few dollars with your friends for a lark, quite another to put so much into it. Was the poor man using up his weekly paycheck? Would his family starve because of his gambling?

Maggie blinked in surprise as her eyes finally rested on the man at the head of the line. He was nicely dressed in a dark suit, his hair cut in a stylish manner that was obviously expensive. There was something about him that seemed familiar. That sandy hair . . .

"Victoria," Maggie said. "Look at that man up at the counter. Does he look like someone we know?"

The clerk must have finished with his tickets at that moment, for just as Victoria looked up the man turned. A thick stack of paper tickets were clutched in his hand.

"Why it's Alan Radford," Victoria said.

"Interesting," Maggie commented. She nodded at Alan as he approached, but he didn't seem to notice. His forehead was beaded with sweat and although he wore a short-sleeved shirt with a tie, the tie was loosened, the top button undone.

"He seems a little preoccupied," Victoria murmured.

Maggie decided to take the initiative.

"Hello, Alan," she said, just as he passed beside her. "Hot today, isn't it?"

Alan's head turned; he blinked. The intense, preoccupied look left his face as he recognized her, replaced by a friendly smile.

"Mrs. Browne, isn't it? And Mrs. Farrington."

Victoria didn't correct the "Mrs." "Please, call me Victoria."

"And I'm Maggie."

They all smiled, the awkwardness of the situation somewhat allayed by years of social experience. Still, Alan shifted his weight from one foot to the other, as he faced the women.

"Picking up your lottery ticket for the big jackpot?"

"The Quilting Bee decided to try our luck," Maggie explained. "Victoria and I are the designated ticket buyers." Her eyes moved to the thick stack of paper slips in his hand. "I see you're trying your luck too."

"Yes." His eyes darted to his hand. "I'm buying for the office myself."

He glanced at Maggie and Victoria, then pointedly checked his watch. "And I'd better be getting back."

With a quick goodbye and assurances that he would say hello to Andrea for them, Alan left the store.

The woman ahead of them watched Alan leave. "Good riddance," she said. "I hope there aren't any more like him up ahead. Maybe the line will move now."

Maggie barely heard her. Her mind was busy digesting this new information. True, Alan was a peripheral figure in Candy's family, but he was married to her only biological child. How did his presence here today figure in the whole picture? And was there any help for Louise in it?

35

Maggie rode through the desert near the HB Ranch. There was nothing like the peace of the desert, the warm dry air, the sightings of the native desert creatures. Even as she thought this, Maggie saw a ground squirrel rear up on his hind legs for a quick look around. He spotted Chestnut and scurried rapidly out of sight, his tail becoming an exclamation mark before disappearing into the hole in the ground. His movement startled a lizard, which also skittered away and disappeared—into a different hole.

Maggie had to laugh. Oh, how she'd needed this break. Ever since seeing Alan at the convenience store, her mind had been frantically thinking of various scenarios that might fit what they knew about Candy and her death. The main problem was that they knew too little.

Maggie halted Chestnut for a moment while she admired the view. The rolling hills were dotted with saguaros, currently sporting their lovely white blossoms. The state flower, Maggie thought with a smile. She remembered once holding on to an A-frame ladder while one of her sons balanced at the top, determined to get a photograph of the flower for a school report. She shook her head slowly, trying to remember whom it was. Bobby, she thought. Or was it Hal? The memory played odd tricks sometimes.

At her gentle command, Chestnut continued his placid

walk along the old trail. An ancient, many-armed saguaro lay just ahead, covered with what must be hundreds of blossoms. There wouldn't have been a need for a ladder there; all the arms sported the large white blooms, including those at eye level.

Topping a rise near the cactus, Maggie noticed the western sky turning a beautiful shade of peach. Soon the bats would be flying out to drink the nectar from the saguaro blossoms, carrying the pollen with them from one plant to another. It was time for her to start back.

As Chestnut moved in a southerly direction, Maggie began to notice the changes in light that forecast the upcoming night. The greens of the plants were deeper, the variations in the browns more obvious. It was a shame Louise didn't ride, Maggie thought. This quiet time was something her friend could use right about now.

But quiet time or no, Maggie's mind refused to be stilled. Someone was using Candy's death for his or her own purposes. Someone might even have tampered with Candy's car, long before all this Angel of Death business even began. But who? Nathan, who needed money to destroy some of this pristine land that she found so renewing? Stephanie, who needed money to reestablish herself and her son in her hometown? Andrea, who seemed to have no apparent monetary needs, but had so far shown little remorse at her mother's death? Or was Bobby's analysis correct? Was Andrea so inhibited she felt a need to keep all her emotions bottled up inside? Not a particularly healthy attitude, but not uncommon.

And now the newest wrinkle in an already pleated fabric. Alan. The man must have a gambling problem. How else to explain his extraordinary purchase at the convenience store this afternoon. She didn't for a moment believe that story about buying them for the office staff. There couldn't be that many people working at his office. She understood that he worked for a small practice, with only two or three partners. There were bound to be secretaries, or executive assistants, as they called them now. And a paralegal or two. But she found it hard to believe that there were even as many as ten people working there, and that made the number of tickets he purchased far too great for the standard office pool.

Maggie reminded herself to ask Hal about it later. Sara had been working in the yard when Maggie left for her ride, and she had been invited to dinner.

Maggie glanced at the sky again. Broad strokes of orange and pink were tinting the sky. But Sara had warned that dinner would be late as the boys had baseball practice. Plenty of time.

Maggie smiled at the thought of eating with her grandsons. They were growing so quickly and they always had interesting things to share with their grandmother. Children were into so much these days. No longer did little boys come home from school, do a few chores, then run off to play. No, today's youngsters were heavily scheduled, with sports, music lessons, computer classes, karate, and even yoga competing for their limited time. Maggie didn't envy Sara her job; her poor daughter-in-law seemed to spend half her life in her mini-van driving the boys somewhere or picking them up.

A coyote topped the hill beyond Maggie, then stood for a moment, staring. Unlike the ground squirrel and the lizard, the coyote did not scamper away. He finished his leisurely examination, then continued on his way. His one concession to the presence of Maggie and Chestnut was to keep his distance.

Once again Maggie smiled. There was a creature in tune with his environment. He knew horse and rider were no danger to him and he refused to let them disrupt him.

Swirls of purple joined the colors in the western sky. Only the upper edge of an orange sun was visible, hidden behind distant mountains. Time to go.

With one last look at the undulating ground leading toward the mountains, she urged Chestnut into a trot.

36

"Did you have a nice ride, Ma?"

Dinner was over, the boys settled in the family room before a rerun of *Gilligan's Island*. Maggie, Hal and Sara sat on at the oak table in the kitchen, lingering over cookies and coffee.

"I did." Maggie poured a quantity of milk into her coffee as she answered Hal. With her busy mind searching for a sensible conclusion to Candy's death, she was afraid sleep would be long in coming tonight. Too much caffeine was the last thing she needed this evening.

"You looked very sad when you rode in," Sara said.

Maggie sighed. "It's nothing specific. I get nostalgic when I ride. And I couldn't help thinking about how quickly we're building up the desert. All this beautiful land is disappearing beneath houses covered with stucco and sprawling golf courses." Maggie smiled at Hal. "No offense, Hal. I know that you enjoy a round of golf now and then."

"None taken."

For a moment they all drank quietly, comfortable in the cozy kitchen. Now that the sun was gone, the temperatures were dropping, and Sara had opened the kitchen windows. A light breeze billowed the curtains, cooling the room and bringing the distinctive scent of the outdoors. In another hour it would be impossible to believe how hot the day had been.

Sara's shrewd eyes glanced over Maggie's face. "Are you and the Bee still thinking about Candy and her relationship with her stepson?"

Hal's eyebrow rose. But unlike Michael, he didn't warn his mother away, or scold her for poking into something that didn't concern her. He sipped his coffee and listened.

"We have been discussing it over the quilt frame," Maggie admitted. "We've pretty much eliminated the three people at the care center that Candy suggested as her Angels of Death."

"She thought three people were killing patients?"

Maggie shook her head, smiling at the incredulity in Sara's voice. "She didn't think three people were committing the murders. At least I don't think so. It's just that she named a suspect to three different people. But she gave each person a different name."

"Oh, dear." Sara pushed the plate of cookies toward her husband, but she didn't take her eyes off Maggie.

"That's one of the reasons no one would take her seriously. The whole thing was far-fetched to begin with, and then with her naming a different suspect each time she mentioned it . . ."

"They dismissed it as the ravings of a crazy old woman," Sara suggested.

Maggie nodded.

"So have you given up?" Hal picked up a cookie but didn't bite into it, waiting to hear his mother's reply.

Maggie looked toward Hal. Was his voice hopeful?

"Of course not." Maggie's voice was firm and she shot a challenging look toward her oldest son. "We can't give up until Louise is exonerated. Right now we're wondering if

Candy's accident really was accidental. And considering the fact that most murders are committed by someone close to the victim."

"You're thinking of Nathan and that subdivision of his, aren't you?" Sara's eyes sparkled. "Does he inherit?"

"Well, of course we don't know exactly what the will says. We do know that Stephanie and Nathan get the house. It was Ken's originally, and they told us as much last Saturday. Anna says Candy told her Andrea doesn't inherit at all. But we don't know that for sure. She said Candy told her she put everything into a trust for Andrea's children, because Andrea was so successful she didn't need any more money."

Maggie's brows drew together as she remembered Alan at the convenience store that afternoon. It was just one more element in an already complicated plot.

"Here's something interesting. A new development, I guess you could call it. Victoria and I saw Alan Radford at the Circle K this afternoon."

Maggie went on to tell Hal and Sara about the lottery pool and their experience at the store. Hal was frowning when she finished.

"I'd forgotten that Andrea was married to Alan Radford."

Maggie's detecting antenna went up. "Do you know him?"

Hal shook his head. "Not really. But I've heard rumors about him. He's not generally liked among his fellow attorneys."

"Why?"

Sara and Maggie uttered the question at the exact same moment.

Hal looked from one to the other, obviously reluctant to

pass on what he'd heard. "I shouldn't be adding to the rumors."

"Oh, come on," Sara urged. "It's not as if anyone will know. It's just us, your wife and your mother."

Hal frowned, but he did answer. "Word is that he bills for many more hours than he actually works."

This information didn't shock either Maggie or Sara. "Is that all?" Sara raised delicately arched brows. "According to Grisham's novels, that's pretty common stuff in law offices. And I've heard more than one lawyer claim that their offices are just like the one in *The Firm*, except for the mob stuff." A teasing smile tipped her lips and her voice cajoled. "That can't be all you've heard."

Maggie had to agree with Sara. Overestimating billable hours didn't seem like something Hal would be reluctant to share with his closest family members. "Is there more?"

Hal took the last cookie from the plate and bit into it. He chewed slowly while Sara and Maggie watched. Maggie didn't think he would say anything more. Lawyers had their ethics, despite numerous jokes to the contrary.

Finally, he swallowed his cookie and finished his coffee. The room was so quiet Maggie could hear dialogue from the television program in the other room. *I Dream of Jeannie* had apparently replaced *Gilligan's Island*.

Hal placed his coffee cup on top of the cookie plate and pushed the little stack of dishes into the center of the table. His voice was quiet when he finally spoke. He didn't want his words to go beyond this room. His sons might be young, but there was no telling what they might pick up from adult conversation. And no way of knowing how much they understood.

"There's some suspicion that he's been borrowing money from clients' accounts. His firm is having an audit done."

Maggie drew in her breath. Now that could be a motive. Most children just assumed they would inherit, not knowing the true details of their parents' wills. Alan might assume Andrea, and therefore himself as her husband, would inherit a great deal on Candy's death. She had been a wealthy woman.

Yes, as a motive, Alan's need for cash was right up there with Nathan's.

"Does he know?" Maggie asked.

"I don't see how he couldn't. If word has gotten to me, then he must be aware of it."

"Oh, my." Sara expelled her breath. "It's just like a TV show. He took money from clients, and now he has to put it back. That's probably why he bought so many lottery tickets."

"But that's so silly." Practical Maggie couldn't understand how that kind of reasoning could make any sense. Certainly not to highly educated adults. "The odds of winning the lottery are astronomical. He must know he can't get the money that way."

Just as Maggie had earlier, Sara saw a motive for murder.

"Maybe. But I'm not sure a gambler would see it that way. However, he could get the money through Andrea's inheritance."

37

Maggie's thoughts whirled as she left Hal's. She hated the idea of Alan as a killer, but once implanted, she couldn't get it out of her mind. With this new information, she had to place him right up there with Nathan as a top suspect. Still, would she be any happier if Stephanie appeared to be the one? Or Andrea?

Maggie decided she was too restless to go home. She needed to talk to Candy's stepchildren. But it was getting late, not a prudent time to stop at Nathan's. With his pale wife and young child, Maggie thought it best not to disturb him. She would call on Stephanie. That young woman looked like someone who would be up late.

Maggie's surmise proved correct. Stephanie answered the door before the sound of the chimes had completely dispersed into the depths of the house.

"Why Maggie. Come on in. Good to see you."

"I'm sorry to call so late." Maggie smiled. "I hoped you'd still be up."

"Oh, it's early yet. And it's so nice to have company. I don't know many people here any more, and I get a bit lonely after Kenny goes to bed." She led Maggie into the sitting room. "Could I get you something? Soda? Iced tea? I have some cookies. Store bought, but they're good."

"Oh, no. Thank you. I'm just coming from dinner at my son's."

Maggie sat at one end of the sofa, and Stephanie settled into the matching chair beside it. "Well, I'm sure glad you stopped by. I keep telling myself I have to try and get back together with old friends, but I haven't yet. And I haven't had the chance to make new ones."

"You'll have lots of friends soon enough."

Maggie almost winced after voicing such a platitude, but Stephanie seemed happy enough to hear it.

"I've been looking for a job."

She flashed a wide smile and Maggie thought how pretty she looked.

"I have a good lead."

"Well, I'm glad to hear it." Maggie didn't have to pretend interest either. She was sincerely glad to see Stephanie's happiness. "What kind of work are you looking for?"

"Well, you know I was majoring in broadcast journalism at ASU before I got married and moved."

"I didn't know that." What Maggie did know was that Arizona State University had an excellent program in broadcast journalism, and the prestigious Walter Cronkite School. "With your lively personality, I think you'd be an excellent television journalist."

"Do you think so?"

Maggie was surprised to see insecurities surface in the anxious tone of Stephanie's voice. Stephanie seemed like such a strong, confident young woman. Yet her forehead was creased in concern, and her hands clasped tightly in her lap as she anxiously awaited Maggie's reassurance.

"Yes, I do." Maggie's voice was firm. She was rewarded by Stephanie's brilliant smile.

"I worked as a deejay in Dallas, but I'd just love to work

in television. Radio just isn't the same." She went on to tell Maggie all about the potential job, the upcoming interview, and her nervousness about it. "I can hardly believe it was Alan who found this interview for me."

"Alan?"

"Yeah, isn't it incredible? He's always seemed kind of standoffish to me, like he thought I wasn't good enough to associate with the likes of him. But it just goes to show . . ." She flashed another bright smile. "You can't always go with first impressions, huh?"

Maggie smiled back. Stephanie was easy to like. Maggie found herself hoping she'd do well in her interview the next day. It was hard to imagine this vivacious young woman could be involved in anything as sordid as murder. But Maggie had come hoping for information.

"Stephanie. How is it going with you and Nathan? About the house and all?"

Stephanie's smile dimmed. "You know how it is with brothers." Then she seemed to realize that Maggie might not. "Don't you?" She sent an inquiring look toward Maggie.

Maggie nodded. "Oh, yes. I have two of my own. And four sons."

Stephanie smiled again. "So you do know. Nathan was upset with me. But it's nothing. He needs some money." A wry smile tugged at her lips. "Everyone always needs money, don't they?"

Maggie nodded her agreement.

"But everything will work out okay. That project of his will get off the ground and then he'll have more money than he knows what to do with."

Maggie wondered if Nathan had suggested to his sister that he would be starting to build in the new development soon. "Did he mention that he's going forward with that?"

Stephanie shrugged. "He said he just needed some money for a short period, so I guess that's what he meant."

Maggie just managed not to sigh. Her impression of Stephanie hovered between an intelligent young woman and an airhead. Which was she?

"How about you, Stephanie? Do you need money too?" Maggie knew it was impertinent of her to ask. It was none of her business. But if she wanted to help Louise, she had to pry. And she had discovered that most people seemed willing to forgive an old woman for being a nosy busybody.

Stephanie was apparently one of the latter. She answered without a second thought. "Of course I need money. Who doesn't?" She laughed, a wry laugh directed at herself. "Can you believe I actually bought some lottery tickets? Tonight's that big jackpot—supposed to hit a hundred million. I know the odds of winning are about one in a trillion, but I thought, why not? Someone has to win, right?"

Maggie joined in her laughter. "I have to admit I bought some too. The Quilting Bee pooled our money, and Victoria and I purchased the tickets this afternoon."

"We should wish each other luck then," Stephanie said. She popped up out of her chair, stepped up to Maggie and offered her hand. They shook.

Stephanie returned to her chair, folding one leg beneath her as she settled back against the patterned upholstery. Maggie had to remind herself that this was a grown woman with a young child. At the moment, she looked like a teenager in her worn jeans and faded T-shirt, her eyes sparkling with excitement at the possibility of winning the lottery.

"Stephanie, if you need money, why not just let Nathan sell this house and use your share of the money to get a place of your own? This is a popular neighborhood; the house should bring a good price."

Stephanie eyes lost their glow, and her expression became serious. Her poignant gaze roamed the room, taking in the paintings on the walls and the books and artifacts on the shelves. She sighed lightly before turning back to Maggie.

"I know we have to sell the house and split the money." She clasped her hands and set them in her lap. "Intellectually, I know it. But we grew up in this house. Of course it's changed a lot. But right now, I need to just be here. With Kenny. It feels right." Her gaze dropped to her folded hands. Maggie barely heard her next comment. "I just got a divorce."

"I heard. Was it difficult?" Maggie's voice was sympathetic. It wasn't hard to express sympathy for this cheerful young woman. Maggie hated to see her as down as she was at this moment. Especially after her earlier excitement.

"It was rough."

Stephanie paused and Maggie wondered if she would say more. She didn't.

"Being here now . . . It feels good. It feels safe and comfortable. And that's important for Kenny."

Maggie nodded. She understood. And while she was curious about Stephanie's married life, Maggie couldn't see any connection with Candy or her sudden death. So she didn't want to pry.

"You're giving him a connection to his family. To your own childhood."

Stephanie smiled. "You do understand." Her smile widened. "And now, this chance for a job. A great job. I'm so excited."

Maggie was glad to see Stephanie's mood return to its earlier level. She rose from the sofa. "I'd better go. You'll need your sleep so you can dazzle them tomorrow."

Stephanie stood as well, but she laughed at Maggie's words. "I'm so excited, I don't know how I'll sleep."

"Then you can spend some time deciding on what to wear." She and Stephanie laughed.

As they reached the doorway, Stephanie took her hand.

"Maggie. Thank you."

Maggie didn't have to ask what she meant. Stephanie needed someone to believe she could succeed. Maggie wondered again what her marriage must have been like. Happily, she had gotten out of it before it broke her spirit.

But some things left invisible scars. Could her need for money, along with a mother's natural instinct to look after her child, have pushed her to try murder?

38

Maggie didn't sleep much, her mind busy during the restless night, thinking of Candy's relatives. Andrea, Alan, Nathan and Stephanie. What a group of needy people they had turned out to be. Not just needy for money, either, but for love and commitment.

With her head filled with murder, fraud, and personal relationships, Maggie forgot all about the lottery until Victoria brought it up on their drive to St. Rose. She and Victoria had made copies of their tickets the day before, and while Maggie headed north for her ride, Victoria delivered them to the other Bee members.

No one else forgot to watch the drawing. So everyone was full of regret that morning as they gathered around the quilt frame. While none of their tickets had won, the morning news reported that one winning ticket had been sold.

"In Casa Grande," Edie reported.

"I'm sure they need the money more than we do," Victoria said.

South of Phoenix, Casa Grande was a dusty desert town that often won the dubious honor of having the hottest temperature in the U.S. It was as far removed from affluent Scottsdale as South L.A. was from Beverly Hills.

"It was quite an experience for me, helping Maggie get our tickets," Victoria said.

Maggie agreed. "It was interesting. The woman ahead of us grumbled that her wait was ten times longer than usual to purchase her weekly ticket."

"I'm surprised she didn't get it earlier in the week, then," Clare commented. "The last day is always the worst when the jackpot is high. If she's a regular she should know that."

"The real problem was a man buying two hundred tickets."

The Bee members all exclaimed over this, as Maggie had known they would.

"What a waste of money," Edie declared.

For once, everyone agreed with her.

"I hope he wasn't using his family's food money." Anna's voice reflected her anxiety over any children going hungry because of their father's gambling.

"That is definitely an example of someone with a gambling problem," Edie said. "I don't have any difficulty with people who buy a ticket or two, but two hundred! Did the man look like he could afford it?" she asked.

Victoria nodded. "Oh, yes. He was a businessman, very nicely dressed."

Maggie stopped stitching so she could observe the reaction to her disclosure of the man's name. "It was Alan Radford, Andrea's husband."

"No!" Clare's interest was immediate. "Did he say anything to you?"

"I don't think he even saw us, at first," Victoria replied. "Maggie nodded, but he didn't even notice. She had to call out. He seemed preoccupied."

"I thought he looked worried," Maggie inserted. "He claimed he was buying tickets for an office pool, but I don't see how all those tickets could have been for his small office."

"Well, at least we know he can afford it," Clare remarked. "That house of theirs is worth a bundle." She looked toward Edie. "But I agree with you. I have heard that a lot of the people who spend too much on things like the lottery can't afford it. They're living on the hope of quick riches." She finished off her thread and reached for the scissors. "But at least he wasn't spending his family's food money on gambling."

"That may be true in his case," Edie said, "but you can't always tell either. My Uncle Jerome always looked like a successful businessman. I remember visiting his house and it was nicer than ours. And all the time he was stealing from his company's funds to support his gambling. And that was back before there were state lotteries and Indian gaming. I hate to think of what would have happened if he'd lived a little longer."

Maggie was sympathetic. "I didn't know about your uncle, Edie."

"That's why I've never been happy about all the Indian casinos going up around here."

"That's why he looked so familiar!"

Anna's statement drew everyone's attention.

Maggie looked at her in surprise. "Who looked familiar?"

"Alan Radford. When I saw him at the funeral, I kept thinking he looked so familiar. I thought maybe I'd seen him at church. But your mention of the Indian casinos reminded me."

Anna surprised them with her comment.

"You go out to the casinos?" Maggie tried to picture diminutive and conservative Anna Howard gambling in a casino. The image boggled the mind, but proved that you just never knew about another person.

"My daughter takes me to Fort McDowell sometimes. We play bingo." Anna took a last stitch and busied herself making a knot. "Back home we had bingo at St. Theresa every Wednesday night. What fun we had." She pulled her knot into the batting, sighing with remembered pleasure.

"It's a shame the way the churches used to encourage gambling," Edie grumbled. "At least none of the churches around here have bingo."

But Clare was more interested in the previous topic. "You've seen Alan at the casino?" She looked toward Anna.

"Yes. I see him all the time. But there he's always so intense. I guess that's why I didn't recognize him."

"Intense?" Victoria asked.

"Oh, yes." Anna was definite in her answer. "Concentrating. You know. He plays at the high stakes poker table."

Clare was obviously fascinated. "How high?"

But Anna didn't know. "I just play bingo, and I don't know a lot about anything else."

"Do you think Alan might be like your uncle, Edie?" Maggie asked.

"I'd say so." Edie's voice was firm.

"Maybe that was what he and Nathan were arguing about at the funeral," Clare suggested.

Maggie had to smile at the eagerness in her voice. She felt sure Clare would soon be dredging up a mystery plot that included gambling. She wasn't disappointed.

"You know I remember this book . . ."

Maggie couldn't help it. She burst out laughing. There were chuckles and smiles from the others. Clare looked around; although her cheeks turned pink, she smiled too.

"Well, I read a lot, and I remember the stories pretty well."

"Yes, you do." Maggie enjoyed providing a few encouraging words, especially when they were true.

"So what was this book about?" Victoria prompted.

"Well, the victim was a wealthy older man, and everyone thought his young wife killed him."

"Too bad Candy didn't have a young husband," Edie suggested. Sarcasm laced her voice. "What does that have to do with gambling?" The others shushed her.

Clare went on. "There were two children too, and the daughter was a gambler. She had a good job and lived like it, but it turned out she was deep in debt. She had borrowed from a loan shark and when he threatened her, she killed her father. For the inheritance."

"Oh, how awful," Anna said. "I'm sure I didn't read that one. I don't think I would have enjoyed it."

"Are you trying to say you think Andrea killed Candy for her money?" Edie inquired. "But it was Alan they saw buying the tickets."

"Yes, that is a problem," Clare agreed. "In the book, the daughter tried to make it look like her brother was the one with the problem. She hid slips and receipts and things in his house."

"I don't think that book is anything like this, Clare."

Louise had been more animated this morning than she had been for the last several days, and Maggie was glad to see it. But this last comment was uttered in what Maggie could only describe as a depressed tone.

"We don't even know for sure if Candy was murdered," she reminded them. "Despite what I thought I saw. She could have thrown a blood clot. It often happens after a trauma like an auto accident."

The others met this with silent reflection.

"I don't know." Maggie spoke slowly. Her mind was still working on the problem. "We still don't know if that was really an accident. And I'm not sure a blood clot would have sent the police around to see us twice." Or made Michael tell her to stay away, she added to herself.

Maggie remained silent while she traveled her needle to the next spot in the feather design. She didn't know if she should tell the others what she'd learned from Hal last night. He'd been so reluctant to share what he claimed were merely rumors. As she started to gather stitches on her needle, Maggie spoke again.

"Suppose Alan has a gambling problem, and thought they would get a large inheritance when Candy died."

"But he and Andrea both have excellent jobs," Victoria protested. "Careers. They have that beautiful house, in an expensive neighborhood. They even have a live-in nanny."

Maggie frowned. "But don't you see? All of that costs a tremendous amount of money. And people with high paying jobs often have expensive tastes. It's not hard to spend money."

"Especially if he's a gambler," Edie added.

There were several nods of agreement.

"I still think Nathan is a better suspect," Anna decided. "We know he needed money to save his business. And his wife is pregnant."

"And that Stephanie," Edie added. "She's a tough one. Lost everything in the divorce."

Maggie had to smile. "You're just going for the evil stepmother theory."

Edie and Anna turned quizzical looks Maggie's way.

"Evil stepmother?" Anna asked.

Maggie nodded. "Candy inherited from Ken for her lifetime. They might think whatever he left was rightfully theirs. Knowing Candy, if they had asked her for a loan, she probably would have said no. She believed in working for what you got. But since they needed the money so badly, and they figured it was rightfully theirs anyway, they decided to kill the evil stepmother."

"Like *Murder on the Orient Express* only with two people?" Victoria laughed, but the others looked more somber.

"I like Stephanie," Anna said.

Anna's head was down, her eyes on the stitches she was taking. But Maggie thought that Anna's voice wouldn't have sounded any louder if she had been sitting up tall and looking right at her. Anna just didn't want to believe ill of anyone, but especially someone she knew and liked.

Before any more comments could be made, Maggie jumped up from her seat. Her needle was left dangling over the side of the frame, swinging by its thread like a tiny pendulum. Maggie had been facing the door. Now, as she hurried out, everyone turned to see what had caught her attention.

39

While the others wondered what had gotten into Maggie, Maggie was greeting Andrea in the courtyard.

"Hello, Andrea. What brings you here again so soon? Were you looking for us?"

"Ah, no. I came to see Father Bob."

Andrea looked embarrassed and Maggie was sorry to have asked. The poor girl was probably meeting with Father for some counseling.

"I thought I'd have some masses said for mother." Andrea looked toward the church doors and blinked rapidly a few times. "I stepped inside for a few minutes. It's so peaceful there."

The wistful tone of her voice alerted Maggie.

"I guess your life is pretty hectic right now."

"Yes. Yes it is."

Andrea seemed to shake herself. Anyway, Maggie's keen eyes saw a transformation. The tired, almost languid young woman metamorphosed into the capable businesswoman Maggie had met previously. Maggie was reminded of Bobby's assessment of his old friend; for the first time she felt he must be correct. Andrea was doing her best to offer a cool demeanor to the world.

Maggie put her arm around Andrea. "Bobby really enjoyed seeing you again. He said you two have to get together more often."

The sides of Andrea's lip quirked upward. As a smile, it was not perfect, but Maggie was encouraged by the effort.

"I'd like that." Andrea took a creased tissue from her pocket and blew her nose. "Sorry."

Maggie patted her hand. "You don't have to apologize. You just lost your mother."

"Thank you for everything." This time Andrea's smile was sincere. "You and the other quilters have been wonderful." She checked her watch. "I really must be going. It was very nice of you and the other women to help with mother's sewing room. I stopped by yesterday and saw all that you did."

"We left most of the fabric boxed to pick up later. We thought we'd get someone from the Senior Guild with a truck to help us."

Andrea nodded. "I guess there's no hurry now that Stephanie is living there. I told her she could use mother's things for now. A lot of the furniture was hers, you know. She and Nathan can fight over selling the house."

"So Nathan still wants to sell."

Andrea nodded. "He's having some cash flow problems."

"So I understand."

Andrea looked sharply at Maggie. "It can happen to even the best of businessmen."

Maggie was surprised at the vehemence in Andrea's statement. Was her business too having cash flow problems? Or was she thinking of her husband's situation?

Maggie put her hand over Andrea's. The younger woman was clutching the strap of her shoulder bag so tightly, her knuckles had gone white.

"You should give yourself time to grieve," Maggie said.

"It's very hard to lose a parent, and this is the second one you've lost. You should take some time off, play with the children, take a short vacation."

Andrea's shoulders slumped and Maggie thought she was about to say something important. But she straightened again almost at once.

"It's nice of you to be so concerned, Mrs. Browne, but really, I'll be fine. I couldn't possibly get away right now. Or Alan either. It's always a strain on a marriage when a major event like this occurs. We'll be just fine."

Before Maggie could pursue this interesting new line of discussion, Andrea checked her watch again.

"I have to get home. Alan's car is in the shop and I have to pick him up for lunch at mother's. Ah, Stephanie's. Alan said Stephanie insisted we come for lunch today."

Andrea seemed flustered, but Maggie wasn't sure if it was because of her error about ownership of the house, or because she was running late. Or something else.

But then Andrea's phrasing penetrated Maggie's consciousness.

"She insisted?" Maggie asked.

Andrea laughed. "That's what he said. Alan says she's trying hard to make friends since she moved back here so we have to make the effort."

"I'm glad. I like Stephanie. It will be hard for her starting over again, and friends like you and Alan will be important." Maggie smiled at her. "You're looking well today. I'm glad to see it."

Maggie thought Andrea blushed. Perhaps she and Bobby were wrong about trouble between Andrea and Alan.

"Alan's been very solicitous. I think he's trying to make up for his boorish behavior at the reception on Monday afternoon."

Maggie patted her hand. "I'm glad for you."

Andrea smiled. "I have to go. Tell Bobby it was great seeing him again."

At that she turned and walked rapidly toward one of the gates leading out to the parking lot.

40

Maggie returned to the Quilting Bee room, her steps much slower than Andrea's. The other quilters had used the time Maggie was gone to great advantage. They had just begun to remove the pins that held it in the frame when Maggie walked in. With wide smiles, they showed off the finished nine-patch quilt.

"It's done!" Victoria added a smile to the announcement.

Maggie, temporarily distracted from thoughts of murder, admired the quilt. "It looks wonderful."

The others stopped their work momentarily, joining Maggie in her examination of the quilt. No matter how much they saw it during the quilting process, a finished quilt always looked different—much lovelier.

As Maggie made a comment about how someone was sure to fall in love with this quilt and bid the price up, she stepped forward to help remove it from the frame.

"We saw you talking to Andrea," Victoria said.

"What did she say?" Clare immediately asked.

Everyone was eager to hear a recap of Maggie's conversation. It only took her a few minutes to recount it.

"She's having family problems?" Clare asked as Maggie finished.

Maggie nodded. "Sounded that way to me. But she

didn't specify what the problem might be."

"I wonder about that cash flow comment," Victoria said.

"So did I." Maggie took a final pin from the edge of the quilt and put it into the cookie tin they used to hold them.

"But the thing that really bothers me is what she said about her luncheon engagement," Maggie said. "The idea that Stephanie insisted on having the two of them for lunch."

"That's right." Clare held the wooden slat that comprised one side of the frame steady while Louise finished unpinning the final edge. "You said that Stephanie was looking forward to that interview today."

"Maybe her interview is over and that's why she wants them there," Louise suggested. "To thank Alan and let them know how it went."

Maggie was glad to see Louise taking an interest in their discussion. Even if she was wrong in her supposition.

Maggie shook her head as she spoke. "I know she told me it was right after lunch. She said she was sure she wouldn't be able to eat a thing and I warned her to have something. Wouldn't do to faint during your big interview."

The quilt was now out of the frame. They took another moment to admire their handiwork before working together to fold it into a manageable bundle. Someone would take it home and apply the binding before it joined the other finished quilts in the closet.

"I'm really worried about Andrea," Maggie admitted, placing the folded quilt on the long table at the side of the room.

With the quilt finished, and another top not yet chosen, the women stood or sat, their hands lying still and empty at their sides or in their laps.

"But why, Maggie?" Anna didn't understand Maggie's concern.

"I discussed it with Hal and Sara last night. Just as we decided here this morning, last night we decided Alan might have a gambling addiction. And I'm sure we must be right, after what Victoria and I saw at the store, and what Anna reported about seeing him at the casino. Then Hal admitted there are rumors in the legal community that Alan has been 'borrowing' from clients' accounts. I wasn't going to say anything because Hal didn't want it getting around. But his firm is supposed to be bringing in auditors this week or next."

"Oh, my." Anna's comment was little more than an exhalation of breath.

"Just like Uncle Jerome," Edie muttered.

"It sounds just like a book I read," Clare said. But this time, no one laughed. This was serious business. "The lawyer was stealing from his clients and hiding the money in off-shore accounts. He planned to run off with his young girlfriend. But first, he was going to murder his wife."

"I don't think Alan has a young girlfriend," Maggie said. "At least nothing we've heard or seen seems to point that way. But I'm very worried about the possibility of his harming Andrea." She couldn't bring herself to use the term "murder." "I'm thinking that if he did kill Candy, he did it thinking that they would inherit a lot of money—through Andrea. Being her husband, he would be able to get his hands on it. But we discovered from Anna that Candy left everything in a trust for Andrea's children."

Anna had tears filling her eyes. "She left everything to the children because she said Andrea had done so well with her business. It's supposed to be worth several million dollars."

Maggie nodded. "And unless she has a will leaving everything to the children too, all of Andrea's assets will go to Alan if she dies. People as young as Andrea don't usually have wills, or set up elaborate trusts for their children. They're young and they don't want to think about dying."

"And if his law firm is bringing in an auditor, he'll be getting desperate," Edie said. "He probably thinks he can replace what he took before the audit."

"Shall we call the police?" Anna asked.

"I doubt there's anything they can do," Maggie said. "Think about it. All we have is a lot of speculation, even if it is logical."

"We should go over there." Louise didn't offer this as a suggestion. She was already picking up her purse and passing handbags out of the closet to the others.

As they hurried out to the parking lot, Anna asked what they would do if they arrived to discover Stephanie having lunch with Andrea and Alan.

Edie answered. "We'll just tell them we finished the quilt this morning and decided to pick up the rest of the fabric Andrea donated to the Bee."

Maggie congratulated Edie on her quick thinking. Louise too nodded her approval.

"I hope we're wrong," Maggie said, as they climbed into Louise's van. "But maybe we should all say a little prayer on the way over."

41

"No one's here."

Anna's soft voice broke the tense silence. The Quilting Bee members stood clustered at the front door of Candy's house while Maggie pressed the bell for the fourth time. There was no response.

Clare sounded relieved. "Andrea must have made a mistake about where they were having lunch."

But Maggie was not comforted by the continued silence from the house. Neither was Victoria. She had walked around the side of the house hoping for a view of the garage.

"There's a car parked over here," she said as she hurried back to the others. "A silver Mercedes. Is that what Andrea drives?"

No one knew. But Maggie was waiting no longer. She reached into her purse.

"I still have the key Andrea gave me. We can go in to get the fabric we left boxed up on Saturday," she added, as she stepped forward and inserted the key into the lock. "As long as we're here."

The house seemed steeped in doom after the brilliant sunshine outside. The women all stepped into the foyer, pausing there as their eyes adjusted. Only the dull hum of the air conditioner broke the heavy silence.

Maggie cleared her throat. Her pesky intuition told her something wasn't right. Once again she saw the swooping owl that had haunted her thoughts for the past week. Was it her miniscule amount of Indian blood that refused to let go of that image? And the doom it implied?

Maggie shook her head to clear it of such unwelcome thoughts. With firm resolve, she strode into the house. She would not be intimidated by flying fowl. "Let's just go on to the sewing room and get those boxes."

The others followed.

In the hall leading to the bedrooms, all the doors stood open. Edie nodded with satisfaction as she noted this fact. "It's more efficient for the cooling if you keep all the doors open this way," she informed them.

"Not perfect if there's a fire though," Victoria said.

Maggie had reached the sewing room door, but she didn't go inside. As the others came up behind her, they realized that while she stood in front of the sewing room door, her attention was caught by the room across the hall.

All eyes turned in that direction. Anna and Clare gasped at the same moment that Maggie and Louise rushed into the room.

Andrea Radford lay on the bed in the master bedroom, seemingly asleep. But Maggie knew she was too carefully arranged for an afternoon nap. Lying on her back on the far side of the bed, she still wore the linen dress she'd had on earlier at the church. Her leather pumps remained on her feet, her legs covered by hose. Her hands lay across her waist, one over the other.

As they entered the room, Maggie noticed the prescription bottle on the nightstand—the empty prescription bottle. She looked quickly to Louise, who was already beside Andrea, feeling for a pulse.

"Is she . . . ?" Maggie couldn't bring herself to finish the sentence.

"No. Call 911."

Reluctant to pick up the bedside phone, Maggie called to the others, still clustered at the door. "Someone go to the kitchen and call 911. Tell them it's a drug overdose." She leaned over, trying to read the label on the orange plastic vial without touching it. "It's valium, Louise."

Edie had a cell phone in her hand and was speaking into it before Maggie had even finished. Maggie stared at her in surprise. Who would have suspected that conservative Edie carried a cell phone? And from what Maggie could see of it, it was one of the latest models.

While Louise tried unsuccessfully to wake Andrea, Maggie looked around at her friends. Anna and Clare seemed ready to cry as they peered at Andrea. Maggie felt certain they were watching her chest rise and fall, holding their own breaths in case hers were to stop.

Edie continued to speak to the 911 operator.

"Don't touch anything in here," Maggie warned. Her eyes darted around the room, looking for anything that might be a clue. Finally, her gaze settled on Louise. "And whatever you do, don't leave Louise alone with Andrea."

Clare, Anna, and even Louise turned startled glances toward Maggie.

Victoria stepped up to Maggie and laid her arm around her shoulder. "It will be all right. We came over so quickly, I'm sure it hasn't been long since she took the pills. She'll be all right."

"What makes you think she took those pills?" Maggie asked.

Everyone looked at Maggie.

But Maggie was resolute. "Andrea had no reason to

commit suicide. She might have felt sorrow at her mother's death, but she wasn't despondent. And remember she has those two young children. I just spoke to her barely an hour ago. She was full of plans for the future." Maggie shook her head. "No, she didn't take those pills, at least not voluntarily."

Clare's eyes widened. "You think Alan gave them to her?"

Maggie nodded.

Further speculation was cut off by the sound of sirens outside. Edie rushed forward to open the door.

42

By the Browne family brunch on Sunday, Maggie and the Quilting Bee had learned most of the story. All of Thursday afternoon had been spent at Candy's house with the police. A police officer had arrived with the paramedics, and Maggie had requested—almost ordered—that she notify Detective Warner immediately about Andrea. He arrived as the ambulance bearing Andrea, still unconscious, pulled away from the house.

Maggie immediately accosted him, then spent the next hour explaining everything that led up to the Bee's visit that afternoon. Maggie acknowledged the detective's professionalism with respect. He listened carefully to everything she said, no matter how outlandish he might think it was. Even when the others interrupted with what they considered clarifications or further pertinent information, he was unfailingly attentive and polite.

By Thursday night, Alan Radford was in the Madison Street jail, charged with the attempted murder of his wife. Michael learned of the arrest and called his mother immediately.

"He'll probably be charged with premeditated murder in Mrs. Breckner's death too, but the county prosecutor is still collecting evidence for that charge. Andrea is doing okay, Ma, and she verified that she did not knowingly take those pills. She thought they must have been in the coffee Alan gave her."

Thanking Michael for letting her know, Maggie immediately called all the Bee members with an update, starting with Louise. Maggie could hear the relief in her friend's voice as they spoke. She always knew Louise was worried behind that brave front she'd been affecting.

All the members were there for the Quilting Bee session on Friday, putting Edie's beautiful Storm At Sea quilt top into the frame. It seemed appropriate somehow to be talking about the apprehension of the suspect in Candy's death while they worked on the quilt top made from her fabrics.

After the Quilting Bee meeting, they paid a visit to Andrea in the hospital. They arrived with an armful of flowers, apologizing for not having time to make her a quilt.

"Don't be silly." Andrea looked unnaturally pale, and she didn't smile much. But she thanked the women with tears in her eyes for saving her life.

Maggie urged her to come to the Browne's Sunday brunch with her daughters. But she called late Saturday to plead tiredness.

"It's going to take her awhile," Maggie told Hal and Sara Sunday morning. "Even if her marriage wasn't going well, it has to be difficult to have your husband try to kill you. Not to mention the fact that he may have killed her mother. But she has those darling little girls to live for, and I'm sure she'll rally soon enough so that she'll be there for them."

While Andrea didn't make it, the Browne brunch that week included many guests. The Quilting Bee members were all there—and the husbands of members—as were Stephanie and Kenny, and Tara and her husband. Nathan was invited, but declined, saying that his wife was not feeling well.

"So, Ma, tell us how you knew it was Alan."

Merrie sat with Tara, the two expectant mothers finding much to talk about. But her voice carried easily across the tables to her mother-in-law, sitting amidst her Quilting Bee friends.

Maggie began to explain. She was getting better at recounting the story. This had to be the tenth time, at least, that she was telling it. And of course, the other Bee members couldn't listen without interrupting. That being the case, it took quite some time to go over all their theories and clues.

"You did good, Ma," Bobby told her. "You too, of course," he added, his gaze moving over the other women in the Bee. "You make a good investigative team," he added with a grin.

Clare almost giggled, laughing with delight at the compliment.

"It was really the information from Hal that clinched it for me," Maggie said. She looked toward her eldest son, sitting beside his wife, his arm draped loosely around her waist. "And Sara's comment on Wednesday night." Maggie's gaze turned toward her daughter-in-law. "You said that if he had taken money from clients, then he probably needed the lottery winnings to replace it before the auditors arrived. But you also said that he could get the money through an inheritance from Andrea."

Sara nodded. "It didn't seem real at the time. I was just theorizing, the way I do when I watch television programs and try to guess the bad guy."

"Maggie knew something was wrong that morning," Clare told them, "when Andrea told her about lunch. She knew about Stephanie being gone, of course, but we all thought it was just a misunderstanding about the time."

Michael replaced the coffee mug he'd started to raise. "But of course, Alan had sent Stephanie on a wild goose chase. There wasn't a job interview; he just wanted her out of the house."

Stephanie nodded. She sat beside Sara, the two women keeping watch over their sons at the children's table.

"I thought he was being so nice to me, finding me such a great job interview and all. And it turns out he was using me." Stephanie had stopped by the church on Friday, anxious to speak to someone about the curious happenings of the previous day. So the Quilting Bee women had already heard her story.

"But Stephanie managed to get an interview anyway." Maggie smiled. "It's your terrific personality, Stephanie. I think it's only a matter of time before we're seeing you on the television news."

Stephanie grinned at them all. "Wouldn't that be just wonderful? Y'all have been so nice to me, too, if I get the job I'll owe it to you."

"Of course not," Victoria told her. "*When* you get the job, it will be because you've worked hard for it."

"But how did Alan get Andrea to swallow all those pills?" Tara hadn't talked to the Bee women or to Andrea, so she still hadn't put all the pieces together.

"He didn't, not really," Maggie said. "It turns out Andrea loves flavored coffee drinks. He gave her an espresso machine for Christmas, and when things were going well between them, he would make up special drinks for her. So she was feeling pretty good when she picked him up for lunch and he handed her an iced coffee drink."

"He drove his car over to Candy's neighborhood and left

it parked nearby," Clare informed anyone who didn't already know. "Then he told her his car broke down and was in the shop so that she had to come by and get him."

"Yeah." Michael picked up the story. "Earlier that morning, he'd parked his car on the next street over from Candy's. A homeowner there ID'd it. He then used his cell phone to call a friend, explaining that his car broke down and he needed a ride home. Gave him a sob story about having to meet his wife and the trouble he'd be in if he was late. Then, once he got home, he proceeded to mix up that valium-laced drink for Andrea."

"She was probably already groggy when they arrived," Louise guessed.

"She doesn't remember a lot of what happened at the house," Maggie said. "But she did recall an odd taste to the coffee. She said Alan told her it was a new brand of vanilla he'd gotten to try. And she also said she was dizzy when she got out of the car. That's about all she remembered."

"That poor girl," Anna said. "But why did he do it?"

"For the money of course." Edie's reply was prompt.

"Oh, I know that. But how could he have thought he would get away with murder? Or even with embezzling from his clients?"

"It was the gambling, I'll bet." Edie didn't have to tell the Bee women that she was thinking of her uncle.

"He was desperate," Michael said. "Arrogant and desperate. Criminals are stupid."

There wasn't much to be said in reply to that. The adults were silent, a few still picking at their food. From the children's table however, came talking and laughter.

"What about Candy?" Louise asked.

Maggie looked to Michael.

"There was definite evidence that she did not die of natural causes." He looked to Louise. "Those petechial hemor-rhages that you noticed, Louise." He paused to nod in her direction. "The medical examiner suspected suffocation, but the real cause of death was cardiac arrest. They think Alan put a pillow over her face. She would have been very frightened, and the stress of that and not enough oxygen, would have been enough to cause her heart to stop."

"But why did they seem to be trying to pin it on Louise?" The indignation was evident in Maggie's voice. While no one had ever admitted that Louise was a suspect, Maggie remained convinced that the questions pointed in that direction.

"There was so much activity at the care home the after-noon Candy died, it was hard to determine exactly who had been with her. Louise being the last one to see her before the staff determined her heart had stopped, she was bound to be a suspect."

"Ah, ha!" Maggie almost crowed in satisfaction. "I knew she was a suspect, even though all of you tried to talk me out of it."

Vince acknowledged Maggie. "I didn't think there was anything in their questions. The police always ask for every little detail, and they ask over and over again. But you were right all along."

"Ma's always right," Bobby averred.

Maggie tried to demur, but her sons and her friends all agreed.

"No one's as smart as Maggie when it comes to solving problems," Clare said. "And that goes for murder mysteries just as much as for problems with quilt borders or designs."

Louise nodded. "Don't know what I would have done without you."

"You would have done just fine, that's what."

"Regardless, I think you deserve a toast," Clare said. She raised her glass of iced tea. "To Maggie. May all friends be as faithful and supportive."

All around the picnic tables, glasses were raised. Even Michael picked up his glass and saluted his mother. She'd done well. But next time . . .

Horrified, Michael checked his errant thought. There wouldn't be a next time. Because next time something happened—if anything else like this happened—he would step in before his mother got so intimately involved. Yes. He would.

Addendum

To make a nine-patch block like those in Candy's lap quilt, you will need nine squares—five from dark fabric (blue, in Candy's quilt) and four from light (white). Cut each square three and a half inches on a side. Sew them into three rows of three squares each using a one-quarter inch seam. The first and third rows will have two dark squares on either end, and a light square in the middle. The second row will be the reverse: two light squares at either end and a dark one in the middle. When these three rows are sewn, stitch the rows together, still using the quarter inch seam allowance, and being careful to match the seams. The finished block will measure twelve and a half inches.

To make a small quilt measuring thirty-six inches by forty-eight inches, piece six nine-patch blocks. Cut six alternate blocks of the light fabric, twelve and a half inches square. These are the blocks in which the women appliquéd a red heart for Candy. Make rows with these blocks, placing one pieced square, then one plain, etc., until you have four rows, each made up of three blocks.

The quilt may be finished with a border. Use the dark fabric (the blue) and cut a border four and a half inches wide. Apply to each edge. Layer and quilt. Bind with the blue.

About the Author

Annette Mahon is an avid reader who always wanted to write novels of her own. She is also a quilter, and enjoys including quilts and quilters in her novels. A native of Hilo, Hawaii, she now resides in Arizona. Visit her website at www.annettemahon.com. Email her at annette@annette mahon.com.

.